MIDDLE EARTH

THE LEVANT

A SHORT HISTORY OF THE MIDDLE EAST

BY

G.S. Willmott

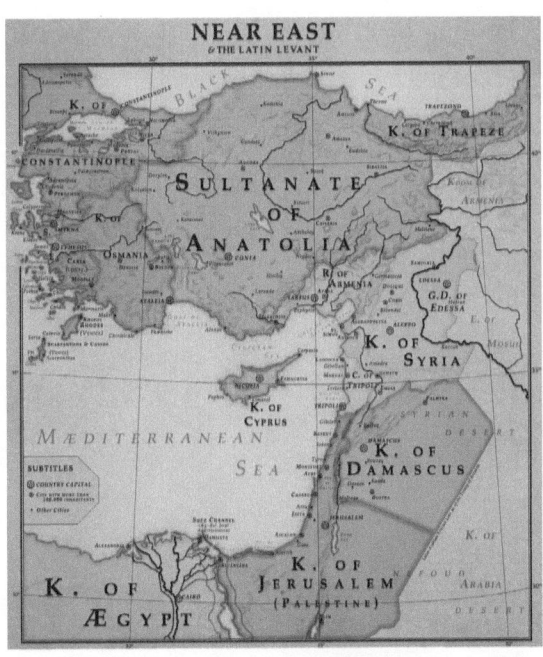

In the Beginning

Chapter 1

Cave Life in the Stone Age

Israel. One Million Years Before Christ

Orr led his men on an important hunting expedition. The snow on the ground had made it difficult to hunt for the past few weeks and consequently his tribe was close to staving. There were twenty men in the hunting party; more than enough to bring down an elephant, which was their objective. They also were hoping to bring back a deer.

Their tools included long spears with flint tips and flint axes.

Orr and his hunting party were skilled and experienced hunters, yet they did not underestimate the difficulty of bringing down such large beast.

The hunting party surrounded the massive animal, which they had lured from its herd and trapped against a steep cliff. Orr threw the first spear. The elephant hardly flinched. The other men threw their spears and by the time all the spears had been thrown and found their mark, the elephant was on its knees. The hunters finished it off with their stone axes.

The hunters butchered the beast and each man was allocated a parcel of meat to take back to the cave to feed his family. The women and children would eat well at last.

How did these early humans communicate with each other during the hunt?

Early humans possessed the ability to hear and produce speech in a way that closely resembles modern-day humans', a recent study has found.

Researchers used high-resolution CT scans to compare virtual 3D models of the ear structures in Homo sapiens and Neanderthals, our closest ancient human relatives, as well as analysing earlier fossils.

They found that far from the traditional notion of caveman grunts, early humans had a similar capacity to produce the sounds of speech as that of modern humans and their hearing system was also as fine as ours, with ears that were "tuned" to perceive those frequencies.

The tribe consisted of thirty men and thirty-five women. There were forty children.

While the men in the hunting party were hunting the elephant and deer, the women were catching tortoises; a delicacy enjoyed by the whole tribe.

The men arrived back at the cave with enough meat to feed the tribe. Vegetable matter was also gathered and consumed.

Orr instructed his group to place the meat at the far end of the cave. He knew it would keep longer as the air temperature was cooler.

Orr's wife Nalda approached him. 'You have done very well, Orr. We will eat well today.'

'Yes, I'm pleased with our efforts.'

Orr led the hunting group out again the following week and this time they hunted deer. Hunting and gathering were an integral part of early Israeli life. The age expectancy was thirty years.

Life as cave people continued for aeons with no real changes occurring until the discovery of bronze.

THE BRONZE AGE
Chapter 2

Orr and Nalda raised five children before they died in their early thirties. The generations continued for nearly one million years.

Their descendants lived close to the cave of Qesem where Orr and Nalda had lived. It became a large city known as En Esur. This city was an early Bronze Age metropolis located in the northern Sharon Plain in the Israeli Plain.

En Esur was established around 3000 BCE and grew to have a population of over 6000 citizens.

En Esur Ruins

En Esur was known for its fine bronze manufacturing. Tin and copper were heated together. As the two metals melted, they combined to form liquid bronze. This was poured into clay or sand moulds and allowed to cool.

Osur was regarded as the finest bronze artisan in the city. His speciality was forging swords. Men from En Esur ordered their swords from Osur and also men from villages far and wide came to him for their weapons.

Osur had been commissioned by the city chief, Irab, to forge him a sword. This sword was to be of the finest workmanship worthy of accompanying Irab into battle.

Irab had held ambitions to conquer Jericho for some time and he had commissioned Osur and other bronze artisans to manufacture swords and spears to arm his army of 1000. This massive project was nearly complete.

Osur was very proud of his work. He sent his young apprentice to Irab's residence to inform the chief his sword had been completed and to ask when Irab would like to inspect it.

'Now. I am very keen to see it. Tell your master to come straight away,' was the response.

Osur was pleased. He wrapped the bronze sword in a fine leather hide and made his way to the chief's residence.

Irab received him as soon as he arrived. 'Welcome, Osur I am keen to see my new weapon, so please unveil it immediately.'

Osur revealed his workmanship with great pride.

'You have done me proud Osur; it is magnificent.' Irab held the sword and tested its weight. It was perfect.

This was the blade that would lead the En Esur army into battle. Irab named the weapon *Fearless*.

Irab soon assembled his army. They had a 50-mile march ahead of them. He anticipated he would arrive at Jericho in five days. Irab had never been to Jericho or even heard much about it, but his spies had informed him that they were intending to invade En Esur. His objective was to rout the city, taking as many prisoners as possible to become slaves.

Irab ensured his army would be well fed on the march using donkeys loaded with millet, lentils and sheep's meat.

At the end of each day's march, they would pitch their tents and light campfires. A meal was prepared for the famished soldiers.

They were required to retire early so that they were prepared for the next day's march.

At the end of the fifth day, Irab estimated Jericho was five miles away.

He dispatched an officer, a general, to ride to within spying distance to determine their defences.

Acob rode his white stallion to within a mile of the city and dismounted. He crawled the remaining mile being careful not to be seen.

What he saw horrified him, for the city was surrounded by a high defensive wall.

Ancient Jericho

He returned to his steed and rode at speed back to the camp to report his findings to Irab.

Acob asked permission to enter Irab's tent. Permission was given.

'What did you discover on your recognisance mission Acob?'

'I am afraid our mission is doomed, sire.'

'What do you mean, doomed? We haven't even begun.'

Acob described what he had seen. He described the wall as impenetrable.

'There must be some way to penetrate this wall. What if we tunnelled under it?' suggested Irab.

'Sire, that would take years, and besides, the people of the city would discover our tunnelling activities.'

'So what do you suggest, general?

'We retreat before they discover our army. We return to En Esur and build our own defensive wall.'

'Let me think about it overnight. I'll call a meeting tomorrow morning and discuss it with the leadership group before deciding.'

Irab was devastated at the news. He had planned the invasion of Jericho for some years and now, when on the verge of what he anticipated was a grand victory, it appeared failure was inevitable.

The following morning, Irab's six officers met in their chief's tent.

'Men, yesterday Acob rode out to ascertain Jericho's defences. What he discovered was this; the entire city is protected by a high impenetrable wall.'

'How high is this wall, Acob?' asked Amman, his second in command.

'I'm not sure but I would estimate thirty feet. To make it worse, it sits on a mound, which is twice as high as the wall. There is also an observation tower.'

'Do any of you have any ideas?' Irab looked over his officers in turn.

The group was silent.

'Well, get your men ready to march back to En Esur without alerting the enemy.'

They began the march under cover of darkness. Food rations were minimal as they were relying on food provided by the conquered Jericho's stores.

Irab and his army were not aware that scouts from Jericho had spotted them. They reported back to their chief, Jehial, who ordered his army to pursue the fleeing enemy.

A bloody battle ensued in which the Jericho army prevailed.

Of the 1000 men that marched out of En Esur, only 400 returned.

Irab survived and he immediately ordered a defensive wall to be constructed around En Esur.

Jericho and En Esur remained at peace for many years with neither willing to attack.

IRON AGE
Chapter 3

1200 BCE

Irab's family consisted of his wife, Batsheva, and twelve children; eight boys and four girls. Large families were common in En Esur, as the more children the better for the household workforce.

The girls helped their mother with running the household, which included cooking. The boys helped their father tend the livestock and maintain the stone house.

The tradition was for the eldest boy to be conscripted into the army.

The eldest boy was Saul. He was a tall strapping young man who had learned the art of swordsmanship from his father at a young age.

Saul had owned a bronze sword since he turned twelve. The recent trend was for iron to replace bronze, but the consensus was that bronze was a superior metal. The Israeli army made the decision to revert from iron to bronze because it was a harder and more resilient metal.

Azrail the master blacksmith agreed with the decision. He preferred working with bronze despite having to mix the two metals to create the alloy. The blacksmith was finishing off what he thought would be his last iron sword. He left the weapon in the coal furnace overnight.

He returned in the morning and when he retrieved the sword he noticed the metal looked different. He cooled the sword with water. The texture had changed— it had transformed into steel. The carbon from the fire had fused with the iron: a new era had begun.

Azrail repeated the process several times, forging an iron sword and leaving it covered by the burning coal overnight. The result was the same each time. He was convinced he had discovered a new metal which would change warfare for forever.

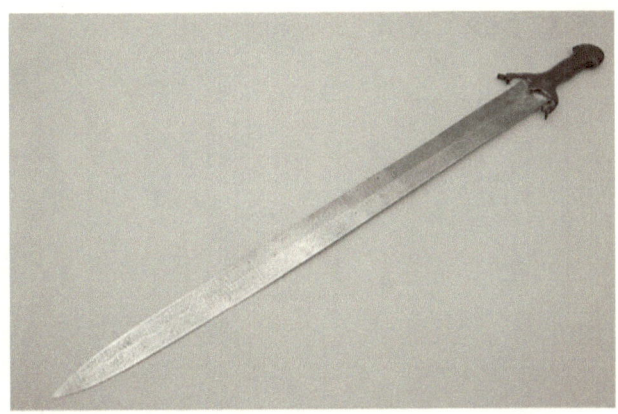
Azrail's Sword

The master craftsman asked for an audience with his chief. He was excited about his discovery. His request was granted and Azrail brought three swords with him to the palace.

Azrail approached his leader, head bowed.

'Why have you requested an audience with me, Azrail, and why have you brought three swords?' his chief asked.

Azrail explained the first sword was bronze, the second was iron and the third was an entirely new metal he had invented. Azrail described the process of manufacturing the new sword and asked for three goats to be brought into the great hall. Goats were sacrificed to the gods on a regular basis.

The sacrificial animals were chosen from the corral of animals housed at the rear of the great hall. All these animals were waiting for their ceremonial fate.

The Nubian goats were understandably nervous. Azrail asked for a soldier to secure the first Nubian to a post used for sacrificial ceremonies.

A guard was instructed to sever the goat's head with the bronze sword. It took three blows.

The iron sword required four blows. Finally the steel sword severed the goat's head with one blow.

The Israeli chieftain was suitably impressed. He ordered Azrail to teach all the blacksmiths in En Esur the art of steel making. It was the chief's intention to equip his army with the new weapons and then march on Gaza and defeat Israel's (Judea's) greatest enemy, the Philistines.

For many years the Philistines had better weapons together with a well-trained army. The Israelites were an inferior foe, beaten in all the battles by a superior enemy. The steel weapons would change their fortunes.

THE PHILISTINES (1186 B.C.)

Ancient Philistine

The Philistines were an ancient people who lived on the south coast now known as the Gaza Strip. Their reign lasted from the 12th century BC until 604 BC. Their mortal enemy was Israel.

Israel was a group of tribes with no supreme leader. Samuel, a highly regarded judge, identified Saul as a potential king who could unite the tribes of Israel. He was tall and was regarded as a great warrior. Saul was chosen as king prior to the first battle when the Israelis used steel weapons. His first battle was a triumph.

The Philistines were devastated. They knew they must hit back with a new weapon themselves. They identified the weapon as Goliath of Gath, a giant of a man. The King of the Philistines, Abimelech, was sure his challenge to the Israelis would bring him victory.

Abimelech's spies had informed him the Israelis had developed a new type of metal to manufacture superior weapons of war. He was reluctant to send his army against a superior enemy.

He instructed Goliath to face the opposing force and challenge the Israelis to a one-on-one duel. The victor's side would become the winner of the battle.

The giant stepped forward from the Philistine army and yelled out his challenge.

'Choose one of your men to fight me. If he wins and kills me, we will be your slaves. But if I win and kill him, you will be our slaves. I dare you to pick someone to fight me.'

For forty days and nights Goliath yelled out his challenge to the Israeli forces but not one soldier accepted the challenge, including Saul's son and heir.

David the shepherd was instructed by his father Jesse to take bread and grain to his three elder brothers who were facing the Philistine army and Goliath.

LAND OF THE
PHARAOHS
Chapter 4

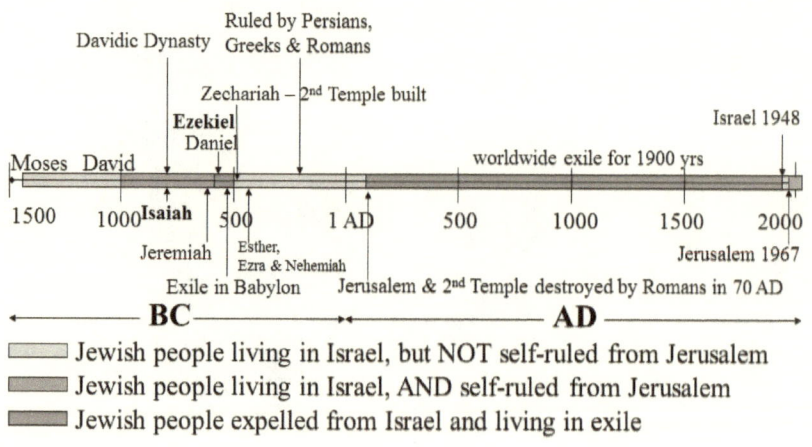

In the Judaic tradition, Moses is revered as the greatest prophet and teacher. According to the book of Exodus, he was born in Egypt to Hebrew parents, who set him afloat on the Nile in a reed basket to save him from an edict calling for the death of all newborn Hebrew males.

Discovered by the pharaoh's daughter, he was reared in the Egyptian court. After killing a brutal Egyptian taskmaster, he fled to Midian, where Yahweh (God) revealed himself in a burning bush and called Moses to deliver the Israelites from Egypt. With the help of his brother, Aaron, Moses pleaded with the pharaoh for the Israelites' release. The pharaoh let them go after Yahweh had inflicted a series of plagues on Egypt, but then sent his army after them. Yahweh parted the waters of the Red Sea to allow the Israelites to pass, and then drowned the pursuing Egyptians.

Yahweh made a covenant with the Israelites at Mount Sinai and delivered the Ten Commandments to Moses, who continued to lead his people while they endured 40 years of wandering in the wilderness until they reached the edge of Canaan (southern Levant). He died before he could enter the Promised Land. Authorship of the first five books of the Hebrew Bible is traditionally ascribed to Moses.

The description of Moses in the scriptures is disputed in archaeological research. There is no evidence of Moses's existence. Exactly when Exodus took place has not been documented. Scholars have placed Exodus taking place ranging over a five-hundred-year span.

Neither do we know the identity of the Pharaoh in the Bible, reported as being Ramesses II. Ramesses is known for his conquests and building projects but not for his cruelty. Historians have found no trace of Moses under Ramesses's reign.

The parting of the Red Sea is also questioned. One theory is that strong winds swept through a brackish lagoon in the Nile Delta (not the actual Red Sea), creating a channel through which runaway Israelites could flee.

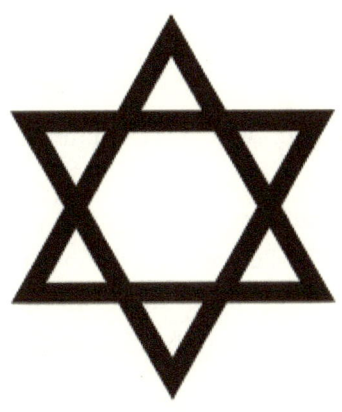

DAVID

Chapter 5

David arrived at the battlefield exhausted, having walked the thirty miles from Bethlehem carrying provisions for his warrior brothers.

He saw the giant Philistine yelling his challenge.

'Why doesn't one of our soldiers take up the challenge?' David asked a soldier.

'You've seen and heard him. No one could defeat that giant.'

'If one of our men steps up and defeats this creature will Saul reward him?'

'Oh yes; not only would the victor receive riches, but he would also receive the hand in marriage of Saul's beautiful daughter.'

'And not one of our warriors will take him on?'

'You've seen him. It would be suicide.'

'I'll do it. I'll kill him and hold his severed head high for all our army to see,' David said.

The soldier shook his head, but said, 'I will go to our king and tell him of your willingness to fight to the death for our country.'

Saul was amazed that a shepherd boy would be willing to fight Goliath.

'Bring the boy to me.'

David kneeled, gazing up at the king, who leaned forward to address him. 'What is your name, boy?'

'I am David son of Jesse.'

'You can't fight this giant Philistine, David son of Jesse. You're not even a soldier—you are just a boy.'

'I have killed a bear and a lion who attacked my father's sheep. This Philistine will be no more of a challenge than those.'

'Then go, and may Jehovah be with you.'

The battlefield was in the Valley of Elah. A river flowed through the valley and the young boy gathered five smooth stones from the riverbank and placed them in a leather bag. He took his slingshot and walked out to meet the giant.

The Valley of Elah Today

Goliath saw the young boy and he laughed. 'Is this the best you have to take on the greatest warrior of all time?'

David stood his ground.

'Come to me boy and I'll slice you up and feed you to the birds.'

'No, you come to me, and with the help of Jehovah I will strike you down.'

David decided to take the initiative and ran towards the Philistine. He retrieved a stone from his bag, placed it in the sling and flung it as hard as he could. The stone hit Goliath on the forehead and the giant collapsed dead on the stony ground. David took the enemy's sword and severed his huge head from the body. He held up the grotesque trophy for both armies to see.

Israel won the battle and eventually David became the most revered king in Israel's history. Saul became jealous of David's popularity with the masses. He plotted to kill David several times, but each attempt failed.

Samuel, the prophet who appointed Saul as king changed his allegiance to David.

Saul was killed in the battle of Mount Gilboa, and David became Israel's greatest king.

Mt Gilboa

King David ruled as King of the Israelites for forty years. He united the tribes of Israel and conquered Jerusalem.

His son Solomon succeeded him, and he too ruled for forty years. He not only acquired riches, but he built the temple in Jerusalem.

David's dynasty lasted for many years.

The House of David

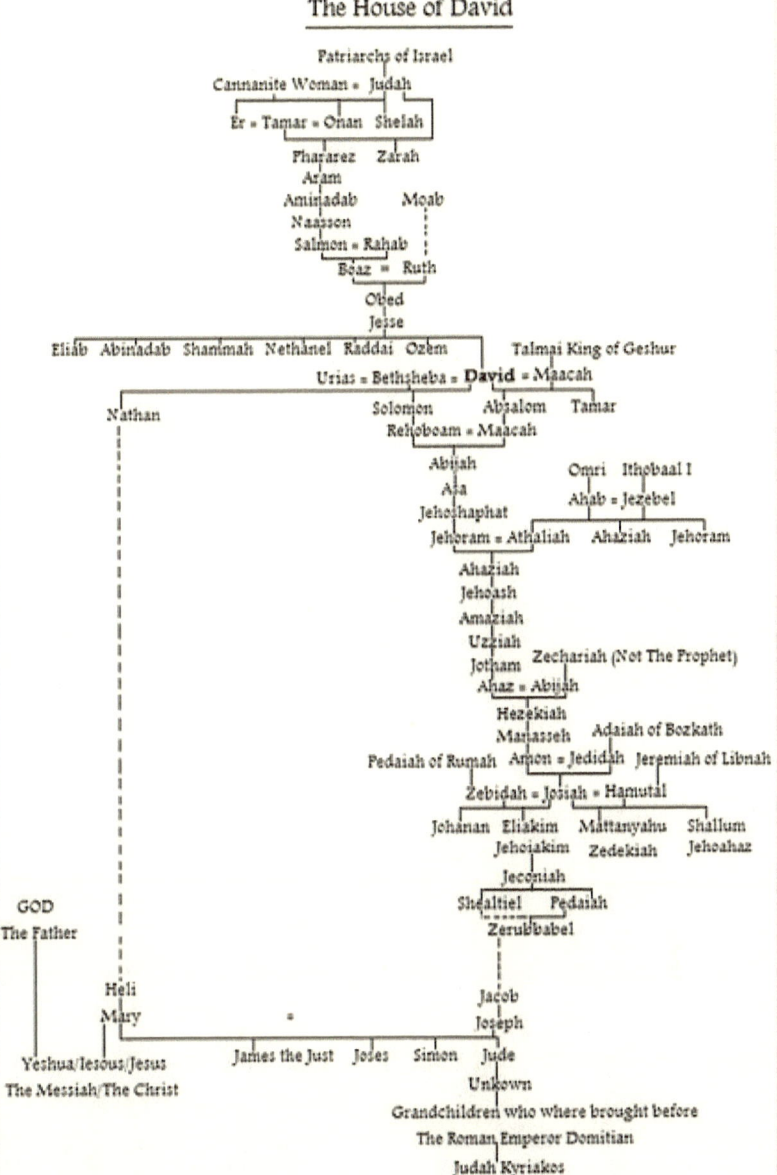

Patriarchs of Israel

Cannanite Woman = Judah

Er = Tamar = Onan   Shelah

Phararez   Zarah
Aram
Aminadab   Moab
Naasson
Salmon = Rahab
    Boaz = Ruth
        Obed
        Jesse

Eliáb Abinadab Shammah Nethanel Raddai Ozem   Talmai King of Geshur

Urias = Bethsheba = David = Maacah

Nathan   Solomon   Absalom   Tamar
        Rehoboam = Maacah

        Abijah
        Asa   Omri   Ithobaal I
        Jehoshaphat   Ahab = Jezebel
        Jehoram = Athaliah   Ahaziah   Jehoram

        Ahaziah
        Jehoash
        Amaziah
        Uzziah
        Jotham   Zechariah (Not The Prophet)
        Ahaz = Abijah

        Hezekiah
        Manasseh   Adaiah of Bozkath
Pedaiah of Rumah   Amon = Jedidah   Jeremiah of Libnah
        Zebidah = Josiah = Hamutal

    Johanan Eliakim   Mattanyahu   Shallum
        Jehoiakim   Zedekiah   Jehoahaz

        Jeconiah

        Shealtiel   Pedaiah
        Zerubbabel

GOD
The Father
                Jacob
    Heli   Joseph
    Mary

Yeshua/Iesous/Jesus   James the Just Joses Simon Jude
The Messiah/The Christ   Unkown

        Grandchildren who where brought before
        The Roman Emperor Domitian
        Judah Kyriakos
        The Last Jewish Bishop of Jerusalem

23

ROMAN RULE
Chapter 6

What have the Romans ever done for us?

Reg: They bled us white, the bastards. They've taken everything we had. And not just from us! From our fathers, and from our father's fathers.

Loretta: And from our father's fathers.

Reg: Yeah.

Loretta: And from our father's fathers.

Reg: Yeah, all right Stan, don't **delay with the point**. And what have they ever given us in return?

Revolutionary I: The aqueduct?

Reg: What?

Revolutionary I: The aqueduct.

Reg: Oh. Yeah, yeah, they did give us that, ah, that's true, yeah.

Revolutionary II: And the **sanitation.**

Loretta: Oh, yeah, the sanitation, Reg. Remember what the city used to be like.

Reg: Yeah, all right, I'll **grant** you the aqueduct and sanitation, the two things the Romans have done.

Matthias: And the roads.

Reg: Oh, yeah, obviously the roads. I mean the roads **go without saying,** don't they? But **apart from** the sanitation, the aqueduct, and the roads…

Revolutionary III: **Irrigation.**

Revolutionary I: Medicine.

Revolutionary IV: Education.

Reg: Yeah, yeah, all right, fair enough.

Revolutionary V: And the wine.

All revolutionaries except Reg: Oh, yeah! Right!

Rogers: Yeah! Yeah, that's something we'd really miss Reg, if the Romans left. Huh.

Revolutionary VI: Public baths.

Loretta: And it's safe to walk in the streets at night now, Reg.

Rogers: Yeah, they certainly know how to keep order. Let's face it; they're the only ones who could in a place like this.

All revolutionaries except Reg: Hahaha…all right…

Reg: All right, but apart from the sanitation, the medicine, education, wine, public order, irrigation, roads, the fresh-water system and public health, what have the Romans ever done for us?

Revolutionary I: Brought peace?

Reg: Oh, peace! Shut up!

Monty Python Life of Brian

Pompey, Jerusalem's conqueror

Pompey was not only a revered politician and close friend of Julius Caesar, but he was regarded as one of the greatest generals of his time.

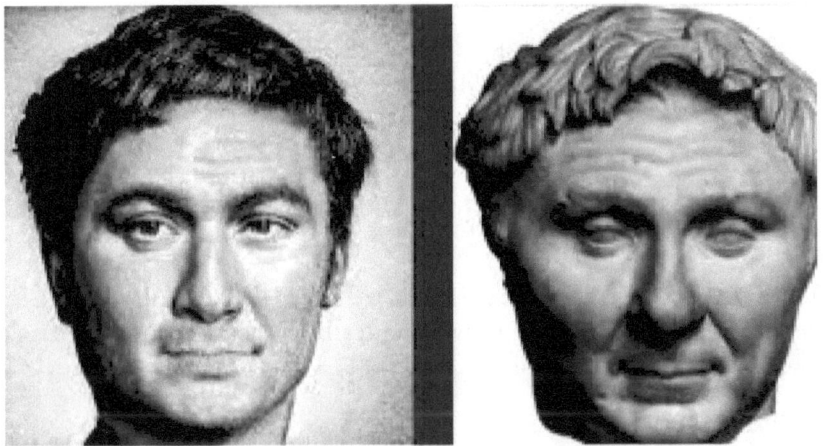

General Pompey Reconstruction

On his return to Rome from defeating Hispania he put an end to the slave revolt led by Spartacus.

The Senate then commanded Pompey to eradicate the pirates of Cilicia who were causing the empire much grief.

Roman Ships Defeat Cilicia Pirates

He was given extraordinary powers for three years to achieve the task. He took three months to achieve his objective.

With the remaining thirty-three months he decided to pacify the eastern Mediterranean.

He began his conquests by invading and annexing Pontus, now known as Northern Turkey, on the Black Sea.

His next conquest was Armenia and then he went on to conquer Syria.

The victorious general then moved on to the holiest of holy's, Jerusalem.

The Israelites had destroyed the two bridges that gave access to the city and the temple.

Pompey decided to attack from the north using siege towers.

The Romans only worked building the towers on the Sabbath knowing they were safe from attack.

Employing massive catapults and battering rams, they breached the city wall, allowing the soldiers to enter immediately. Then the killing started.

Pompey Defeats Jerusalem

When Pompey and his army eventually controlled the temple, Pompey and his senior officers entered the Holy of Holies. This was regarded as a blasphemous act as only the high priest was allowed to enter this chamber.

The treasures, including the sacred vessels, were taken back to Rome.

The Jewish kingdom was annexed by the Romans and now Judea and Galilee had become just another client kingdom.

Initially life in Israel was relatively calm under Roman rule. The Roman Senate had appointed Herod as the Governor of Galilee and the population regarded him highly.

The senate elevated Herod to the position of "client" King of Galilee.

Herod ruled for thirty years under the watchful eye of Rome. He achieved great personal wealth as well as building a grander Jerusalem such as expanding the Temple Mount and his greatest legacy— reconstructing the Temple.

The royal palace was expanded and refortified and many other buildings, including an amphitheatre, were constructed.

Around AD 30 a significant event occurred which would have widespread ramifications for the Roman Empire.

Jesus of Nazareth was crucified for blasphemy for claiming to be King of the Jews.

In 313 AD, the Emperor Constantine issued the Edict of Milan, which accepted Christianity: 10 years later, it had become the official religion of the Roman Empire.

In 476 The Roman Empire fell.

JERUSALEM

Chapter 7

Abu Ubaidah

The siege of Jerusalem (636–637) was part of the Muslim conquest of the Levant and the result of the military efforts of the Rashidun Caliphate against the Byzantine Empire in the year 636–637/38. It began when the Rashidun army, under the command of Abu Ubaidah, besieged Jerusalem beginning in November 636.

1085

The young Frenchman was riding his white stallion through the countryside of Champagne. His parents had given the steed to him for his sixteenth birthday. He imagined himself charging down an enemy, striking all in front of him with his finely forged steel sword, which was also given to him by his parents.

The youth's name was Hugues de Payens and he was the firstborn son and as such would soon become a knight.

His knighthood would be bestowed upon him at the age of twenty-one. Once he was knighted, Hugues courted and soon married Elizabeth de Chappes who bore him a son.

The young knight's mentor was Hugh, the Count of Champagne, a highly regarded knight in Louis VI's court.

Emblem of Hugh, the Count of Champagne

1143

Hugues and his wife were invited to dinner at his mentor's chateau. This was an invitation one did not refuse.

Their carriage arrived at six o'clock and they were greeted by the head butler and shown into the magnificent drawing room where Hugh and his wife greeted the young couple.

It was during dinner that the count invited his young protégé to join him on a sacred trip to the Holy Land.

'As you know, Hugues, the crusade was a resounding success. It is now safe to travel to Jerusalem.'

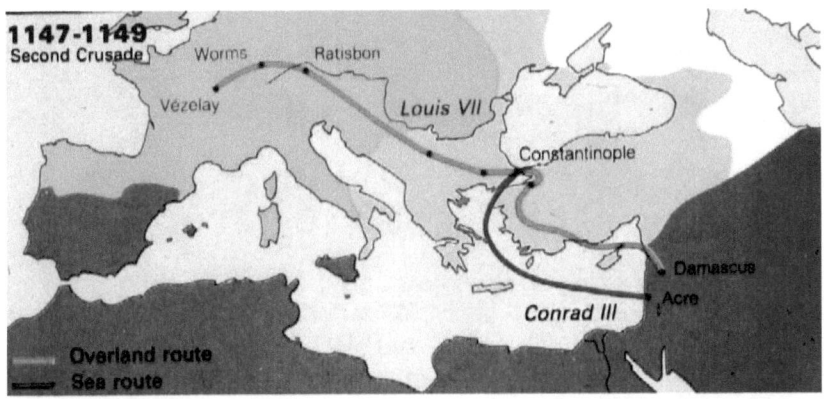

During the First Crusade, Christian knights from Europe captured Jerusalem. The holy city suffered a seven-week siege. Once Jerusalem was captured the Crusaders massacred the city's Muslim and Jewish population. It is estimated over 40,000 Muslims and Jews died.

The count, Henry, decided to return to France because he missed his family, and he feared the estates he left behind had could well have declined.

Before he could embark on the long journey to France he died, falling from a first storey window in his palace in Acre, Israel. A dwarf servant tried to save him but the count was too heavy for the little man to hold. They both fell with the servant landing on top of his master. It was probably the cause of death for the count.

Acre Palace
First Floor Window

The Count's widow remarried soon after his death.

His elder daughter, Alice, was Henry's heir. She married her stepbrother, King Hugh of Cyprus. Therefore, the Champagne lineage continues to this day.

Payens decided to stay on in Jerusalem. He approached the King of Jerusalem, Baldwin II, and requested permission to establish a monastic knightly order based in Jerusalem. The purpose was to protect Christians during their pilgrimages to the Holy Land.

The Knights Templar was formed with eight knights.

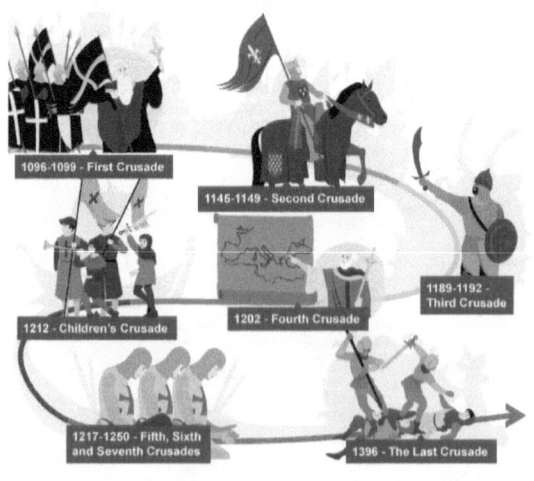

THE KNIGHTS TEMPLAR
Chapter 8

Hugh of Payns had intended for the knights to adhere to a vow of poverty. They in fact became one of the richest organisations in the medieval world.

In 1120, Baldwin II, the King of the Kingdom of Jerusalem, gave the knights his palace, the former Aqsa Mosque on the Temple Mount of Jerusalem, for use as their headquarters. The building was commonly referred to as 'The Temple of Solomon' and so the brotherhood quickly became known as 'the Order of the Knights of the Temple of Solomon' or simply the 'Templars'.

The Knights Templar also became an enormously powerful body with castles and extensive lands in the Levant and across Europe.

Jealousy became the enemy and they were accused of heresy, corruption and performing forbidden practices.

On Friday 13 October 1307 King Philip IV of France ordered the arrest of all Templars in France. His motivations remain unclear, but suggestions from modern historians include the military threat of the Templars, a desire to acquire their wealth, an opportunity to gain a political and prestige advantage over the papacy, and even that Philip actually believed the rumours against the order. To the denial of Christ and disrespect of the cross were added further accusations of promoting homosexual practices, indecent kissing, and the worship of idols.

Initially, Pope Clement V (r. 1305-1314) defended this unsubstantiated attack on what was, after all, one of his military orders, but Philip managed to extract confessions from several Templars including the Grand Master James of Molay. As a result, the Pope ordered the arrest of all Templars in western Europe, and their property was seized. The Templars were unable to resist except in Aragon where a number held out in their castles until 1308.

On Friday 13th 54 Knights burned alive.

LIVING IN THE GHETTO
Chapter 9

Joseph Erzman man was a very successful lawyer practising in Warsaw, Poland. He, like his father before him, was regarded as the common man's saviour. He could have made significant fees representing the rich but he chose not to. He was a true humanitarian.

His grandfather immigrated from Hungry when he was a young man.

Prior to the German invasion, the city had 1.3 million inhabitants, of which 380,567 were Jewish. This was the largest Jewish community in Europe at the time.

The Nazis occupied Warsaw on 29 September 1939. As a result of orders from the High Command, (Hitler) the Jewish population in Warsaw grew significantly, taking Jews from other Polish cities and towns.

October 1940

A Jewish Ghetto was declared ordering all Jews to be moved into the ghetto precinct. The area was surrounded by a high brick wall, which was completed on 15 November 1940, effectively becoming Europe's largest jail. Jewish police guarded the inside of the wall and Nazi and Polish police guarded the outside perimeters.

Jewish Police

The population of the ghetto rose to over 400,000.

Children living in the streets

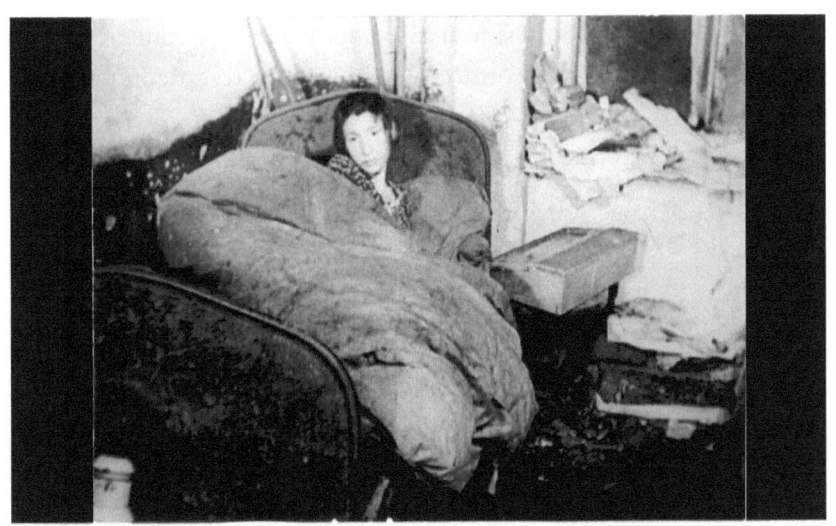

Forced to live in squalor

Everyone lived in fear. The Germans were ruthless.

Joseph, his wife Rosa and their four children; Peter 16, Samuel 14, Ruth 12 and Vida 10 moved out of their comfortable home and resettled into their new home in the ghetto.

The Erzman Family

Erzman home far left

In the family home in their previous neighbourhood, the two girls shared a bedroom, as did the boys. They were large rooms with plenty of space for their possessions such as bikes and dolls' houses.

Ghetto accommodation

The family's new accommodation was one room to house them all. There was no running water or separate bathroom. These facilities were shared with ten other families.

Each day one of the boys would take the toilet bucket and empty it out on the street. The unsanitary conditions and lack of food made for a high death rate among the ghetto inhabitants.

December 1941

Peter decided enough was enough. He planned to escape from the ghetto, find food, and bring it back for his family. He knew if he were caught the Jewish Police would beat him within an inch of his life. He was willing to take that risk. He didn't tell his family what he planned to do. His father and mother would have insisted he abandon his plan if he had divulged it.

Peter waited until 2 am. There was no one in the streets although he knew the Jewish police patrolled all night. He had to be careful. The young man had fashioned a grappling hook from a tin bucket. He was also able to secure a rope thick enough to take his weight.

Peter arrived at the section of the wall he had selected several days before. He had been observing the wall for a number of days without bringing attention to himself, or so he thought. It was isolated and the floodlights did not seem to illuminate the wall as brightly as other sections.

The wall section Peter chose

Peter threw the hook up the wall hoping it would grab hold of the top bricks. All he achieved was the attention of the ghetto police. Peter tried twice more without success and finally he decided to try again the following night. He was conscious the police might hear his attempts. They could and they did.

'What the fuck do you think you are doing, son?'

'I was just exercising sir. I don't get much chance for exercise in the ghetto.'

'Really? Well it looked like you were attempting to escape to me. What do you think, Josh?'

'Yes it certainly looked as if he was trying to scale the wall.'

'I think we'll take you back to the station and interrogate him.'

The two Jewish policemen grabbed Peter by the arms and manhandled the terrified 16-year-old back to a former school that was now a police station.

They placed him in a schoolroom turned interrogation room.

'What is your name?'

'Peter, sir.'

'Your whole name.'

'Peter Erzman.'

'Well, Peter Erzman, are you going to tell us why you were trying to scale the wall?'

'I've already told you sir. I was getting some exercise.'

Josh was standing behind Peter and he hit him on the back of his thighs with a truncheon twice left and right. Peter buckled over and lay prostrate on the floor.

'Now we'll try again. Were you trying to escape?'

Peter knew if he admitted his escape he would be lucky to leave the schoolhouse alive. He also knew if he admitted nothing he would be tortured until he ceased breathing. It was not going to be an easy choice.

The two policemen dragged him up and tied him to a chair. They took it in turns to punch him in the face.

Peter couldn't see out of either eye, and he also had lost his two front teeth. He knew the time had come to tell the truth; he couldn't take any more punishment.

Once he had told his story he was sure he would get a bullet in his head. He was surprised to learn that the two Jewish policemen empathised with his situation. He was released to stagger back to his family's building.

When Peter staggered into the room his father and mother were horrified, as were his siblings.

'Peter, who did this to you? Was it the SS?'

'Father, please let me rest for a while. I will tell you in the morning.'

'You can rest after I clean the blood off your face, darling,' said Rosa.

Rosa used water from their precious water supply and a sock to clean her son's face. Peter lay down on his dirty mattress and fell asleep within minutes.

He woke several times throughout the night but managed to get back to sleep.

Come morning his mother handed him a hot cup of tea—a real treat. His face ached, as did most of his body.

His father approached him. 'Right, Peter; how did this happen?'

Peter described how he intended to obtain food for the family. He also described the interrogation by the police.

'Peter, your motive was very noble but unrealistic. May I suggest you refrain from any other risky actions in the future?'

'Yes Papa.'

There were a few dentists enclosed in the Ghetto, and Joseph approached Dr Cohen, a dentist he had known on the outside.

'David, my son Peter had his two front teeth knocked out by the police. Would it be possible with your limited resources to create false teeth for him?'

'I have been able to do it for others so I see no reason why I couldn't for your son,' said the dentist.

'Will I ask him to see you?'

'Yes, of course. I have a very light schedule.'

Peter visited Dr Cohen the next day and the dentist was able to make an impression with a clay mixture he improvised.

'Come back in a week, Peter, and we will fit you with your new teeth.'

Peter left the dentist's room with a horrible taste in his mouth but he was excited about the prospect of being able to eat normally again.

The week went even more slowly than usual for Peter but at last the day arrived to get his new teeth.

Dr Cohen greeted his young patient enthusiastically. 'Sit down in this chair young man; it's hardly a dentist's chair but it will have to do.'

Dr Cohen inserted a plate he had fashioned. The teeth were carved from dog bone.

'How does it feel Peter?'

'A little strange to be honest but I'm sure I'll get used to them.'

Peter's teeth were never really comfortable, but it was better than having a large gap in his smile—not that he had much reason to smile in the awful place he and his family were forced to live.

July 1942

Between July and September 1942, German SS and police units, supported by the Jewish police, deported approximately 300,000 Jews from the Warsaw ghetto to the Treblinka II killing centre. German SS and police personnel used violence to force Jews to march from their homes or places of work to the concentration point.

Collection Point: Warsaw

They were then forced to board freight cars bound for Malkinia, on the Warsaw-Bialystok rail line.

Jews being loaded onto cattle carriages

When the trains arrived in Malkinia, they were diverted along a special rail spur to Treblinka.

The modus operandi the Germans and Jewish police used was to round up the Jews by cordoning off a city block and systematically forcing the residents out onto the street. They then forced the Jews to march to the holding area next to the train line under heavy guard. As soon as one block was cleared, German SS and police units and their auxiliaries would secure the next block and repeat the process. German SS and police personnel viciously beat and tortured Jews to make them move more quickly; they shot those who were unable or unwilling to move. To lure Jews out of hiding, the German authorities often resorted to announcements that the deportations were over and those who had not been deported would receive food. Starving and unaware that they would be transported to their deaths, some Jews reported, and they too were deported to Treblinka. Toward the end of the deportations, German forces and collaborators systematically searched the then empty apartment houses and workplaces to find Jews in hiding.

In September 1942, as many as 70,000 Jews remained in the ghetto. In January 1943, German SS and police units deported roughly 6,500 Jewish residents of the Warsaw Ghetto to Treblinka. During this three-day operation, 1,171 Jewish ghetto residents were shot and killed.

January 1943

Peter and Sam Erzman did not divulge to their parents the fact that they had both joined the Jewish Fighting Organisation. They knew both parents would be worried about their safety.

On the morning of the 18th of January 1943, German military and auxiliary units entered the Warsaw Ghetto unannounced. The ghetto population expected there would be total deportation. During the Great Deportation, the Jews had no knowledge of where deportees would be sent. This time the ghetto's population refused to report voluntarily because they knew what fate awaited them. Only a small number of people responded to the Germans' calls to file into the courtyards and present their papers for inspection. The Germans tried to pick up those Jews who lacked permits, but since most had gone into hiding, they grabbed whomever they could.

After the summer of 1942 when the Germans deported over 250,000 Jews to Treblinka and Majdanek to be murdered, the remaining Jewish population made a pact to resist the Nazi murders. They decided it was better to die fighting rather than being led like lambs to the slaughter.

1943

They built bunkers and smuggled weapons and explosives into the ghetto.

Both Peter and Sam were selected to become snipers. They showed promise while training as they had hunted for deer with their father many times before the war.

Peter was positioned on the roof of a four-storey apartment building while Sam was placed in the bell tower of a church.

Peter watched a group of German soldiers coming down the street banging on doors and yelling out orders to the Jews to come out and show their papers.

They weren't having much success. The population knew better, and they remained hidden.

The young Jewish sniper singled out the officer leading the group; he aimed for the German's unprotected throat. A single shot from the Mauser and the German dropped to the road. By the time the other soldiers had realised what had happened Peter had shot three more.

Peter descended from the rooftop and quickly hid in the basement of the building. The Germans did not find him.

Sam wasn't so fortunate. He shot two German soldiers but he was discovered and shot.

The SS Commander was furious, and he ordered the burning of the ghetto block-by-block, building-by-building.

Those Jews who escaped the fires were shot and the remainder were burned alive. A total of 13,000 people died. Fewer than two hundred Germans perished.

This uprising was regarded as one of the most significant occurrences in Jewish history.

Some Jews escaped, including Vida, the younger daughter of Joseph and Rosa. Peter joined his brother in the grave.

Joseph, Rosa and Ruth were loaded into cattle wagons packed so tightly they couldn't move. There was no water or sanitation. Cattle would have been treated better.

Treblinka was only a few hours from Warsaw; therefore most of the human cargo survived the journey.

When the train pulled up at the railway landing, SS soldiers were waiting for them. A German officer approached Joseph.

'What was your profession, Jew?'

'I was a lawyer.'

The German raised his Luger pistol and put a bullet in Joseph's forehead. 'We have no need for lawyers here.'

He walked on looking for his next victim.

Rosa and Ruth watched on in horror until they were herded towards the shower house where they were instructed to undress. They were told to leave their possessions, which they could collect once they had showered.

They arrived by rail and departed by the German smokestacks.

A Polish family, the Nowaks, took Vida under their wing despite the danger of being discovered by the SS.

Vida lived in the attic. She felt safe there as there was no reason for the Germans to search the house. The Nowaks were Catholics.

Aleksander, the patriarch of the family, was a headmaster, and he taught Vida all she needed to know. Vida was a very bright student and became much loved by the family including the two Nowak children, Anna and Jakub.

September 1945

The European war had ended. Hitler was dead along with several of his henchmen. Those remaining were tried at Nuremberg where two dozen of them were sentenced to death. The Germans were responsible for 70 million deaths. Seventeen million were murdered in death camps.

Berlin in ruins

Nuremberg Trials

17 Million Fell Victim to the Nazi Regime

Estimated number of victims killed by the German Nazi regime and its collaborators (1933-1945)

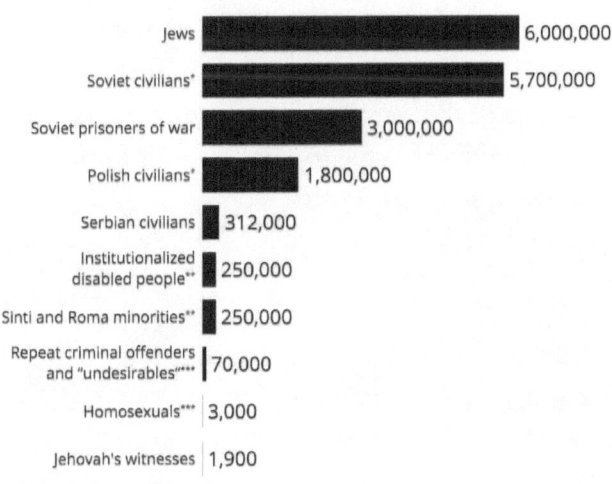

Jews	6,000,000
Soviet civilians*	5,700,000
Soviet prisoners of war	3,000,000
Polish civilians*	1,800,000
Serbian civilians	312,000
Institutionalized disabled people**	250,000
Sinti and Roma minorities**	250,000
Repeat criminal offenders and "undesirables"***	70,000
Homosexuals***	3,000
Jehovah's witnesses	1,900

* non-jewish   ** upper estimate   *** lower estimate
Sources: United States Holocaust Memorial Museum, Dr. Alexander Zinn

EXODUS

Chapter 10

June 1948

Vida

Aleksander asked Vida to come into his study. She had been in this room once before when she first moved into the Nowak household.

'Vida, we regard you as one of our family despite the risk of you staying here. Through the dark days of the war you brightened our lives. Now you are a young woman of eighteen, I think it is time to think of your future.'

'What do you mean, sir?' Vida asked.

'Your people, the Jewish people, including your entire family, suffered a terrible fate under German hands.'

'Yes, I understand, but you and your family saved me from a similar destiny. Are you telling me I am no longer welcome in this house?'

'Vida you are welcome here always, but Ruth and I thought you might want to immigrate to the new Israel and help build a new nation.'

'I thought the Jews were not permitted to return to Palestine. I heard they are being held in camps.'

'Yes, that's true, although these camps have been largely managed by the Jewish interns. They have also been lobbying hard for the United Nations to allow the Jews to establish an independent state in Palestine.

'The greatest obstacle has been the British Government although the USA and other countries put significant restrictions on the number of immigrants allowed into their countries.'

'I knew some of this, although not all. How does this affect me?'

'I gather you were aware that the British held over 50,000 in detention camps in Cyprus?'

'I must admit I didn't know that.'

'Newspapers around the world were very critical of the British Government. They argued this was no way to treat holocaust survivors.

'Finally the British handed the problem over to the United Nations. The UN General Assembly voted on 29 November last year to partition Palestine into two new states, one Jewish and one Arab. The Jewish leadership accepted but the Arabs didn't.'

'So how does this affect me, sir?' Vida persisted.

'Ruth and I will pay for your travel to Israel and your living expenses for the first two years. If you wish to attend university we will help you.'

'Why are you doing this for me?'

'We want something good to come from the evil that has been perpetrated in our country. You deserve our help, Vida, but if you wish to remain in Poland you are welcome to stay with us.'

'May I have some time to think about it?'

'Of course.'

Vida gave her options some deep thought. On the one hand, the concept of living in Israel among her people did appeal, but it also raised some fears. Living in another country and not knowing anybody did cause her some anxiety.

Although she loved living with the Nowak family she knew she would need to leave the fold sooner or later. Poland was not a country she wished to live in for the rest of her life. There were too many horrible memories to haunt her.

After a few weeks of deliberation, she decided what to do. She approached Mr Nowak, requesting a meeting.

'Sir.'

'Vida you are eighteen, almost an adult. Please call me Aleksander.'

'Oh yes, of course, Aleksander. I have given my options a lot of thought and have decided to accept your very generous offer. I would like to immigrate to Israel.'

'Excellent, Vida. As much as the family will hate to see you go, we believe this is the best option for you.'

WAR

What's it good for?
Independence that's what

Chapter 11

November 1947

The United Nations voted to partition Palestine, which had been under British rule, into a Jewish state and an Arab state. The ink was hardly dry when clashes broke out between Jews and Arabs.

Sir Alan Cunningham High Commissioner
Palestine

Sir Alan Cunningham was packing his papers and photos into a large sea chest. He and his 3000 troops were due to board the ships which would take them home to their beloved Britain.

Lieutenant Colonel Briggs knocked on the commissioner's office door.

'Can I help in any way, sir?'

'No, James. I'm nearly finished, thank you.'

'Will you miss living here?'

'In some ways yes, and in others, no.'

'What will you miss, sir?'

'I'll miss Jerusalem and the friends I have made, both Arab and Jew.'

'And what won't you miss?'

'The fighting and bitterness between two ancient peoples.'

'Are you sure I can't help you pack up your office?'

'I'm nearly finished. I'll see you on the ship tomorrow.'

Nevasa had hardly pulled out from the dock when the Arab and Jewish forces attacked each other. Both sides committed belligerent moves. One of the most infamous occurrences was the Israeli attack on the Arab village of Dayr Yasin on April 9, 1948.

The news of a brutal massacre there by Zionist forces spread widely and inspired both panic and retaliation. Days later, Arab forces attacked a Jewish convoy headed for Hadassah Hospital, killing 78.

Dayr Yasin Massacre

Sir Alan Cunningham had settled into his cabin and was looking forward to a whisky before dinner when there was a knock on his cabin door.

He opened it to find Lieutenant Colonel Briggs.

'I'm sorry to disturb you, sir, but I have some important news.'

'That's all right James; what is it?'

'Israel has declared its independence.'

'Oh dear. All hell is about to break loose.'

He was right. The following day Egypt, Jordan, Iraq, Syria and Lebanon occupied the areas in southern and eastern Palestine not allocated to the Jews by the U.N. partition of Palestine. East Jerusalem was also captured which included the Jewish quarter of the old city. The reason given for the invasion was to ensure there was law and order in light of the British withdrawal. The Israelis took control of the road to Jerusalem through the Hills of Judaea. There were continual skirmishes between the Arabs and Israelis, but by early 1949 the Israelis occupied the Negev up to the former Egypt Palestine frontier except for the Gaza Strip.

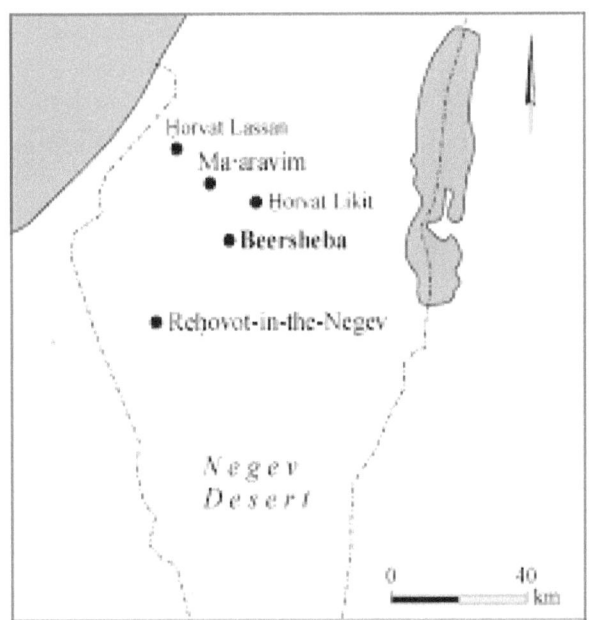

Between February and July 1949, as a result of separate armistice agreements between Israel and each of the Arab states, a temporary frontier was fixed between Israel and its neighbours. In Israel, the war is remembered as its War of Independence. In the Arab world, it came to be known as the Nakbah Catastrophe because of the large number of refugees and displaced persons resulting from the war.

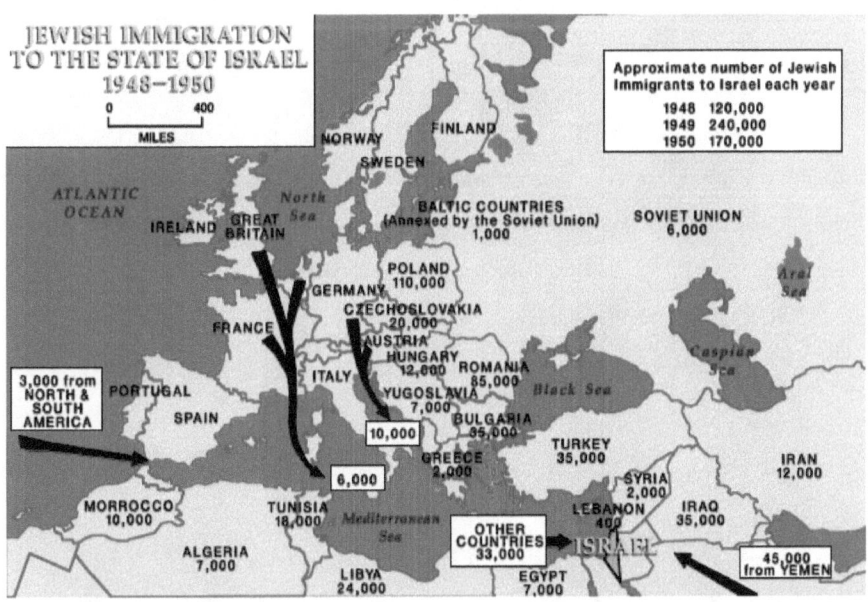

May 1949

Vida was taken to the Warsaw Railway Station accompanied by the entire Nowak family. This was the same station that transported thousands of Jews to Treblinka and their deaths.

Although Vida was sad to be leaving she was looking forward to her new life.

Her journey would take her 1600 kilometres through Czechoslovakia. Austria, Hungary and Yugoslavia. She would then board a ferry to Haifa, Israel, from Athens.

Aleksander had arranged for a senior member of the Bar'am Kibbutz, Joseph Abrams, to meet the young woman and take her to the kibbutz where she would live and work.

Bar'am is a kibbutz in northern Israel. Located approximately 300 metres from Israel's border with Lebanon near the ruins of the ancient Jewish village of Kfar Bar'am, Bar'am National Park is known for the remains of one of Israel's oldest synagogues.

Ancient synagogue

Bar'am Kibbutz 2010

The journey from the port city to the kibbutz took only an hour and a half. Along the way Joseph questioned Vida about her experiences in the ghetto.

'Vida, I believe you are the sole survivor of your family?'

'Yes, I'm afraid so. The Germans killed my father and mother and my two brothers and my sister.'

'I can assure you the members of the kibbutz will become your new family.'

'I hope so. I do feel alone.'

'We have arrived at Bar'am,' Joseph said, a while later. 'Welcome. I will arrange a dormitory for you and in the meantime I suggest you go to the great hall and have a cup of coffee. I would like to introduce you to Adam who has been here from the beginning. Adam will take you to the hall.'

Vida turned to the stranger Joseph indicated.

He smiled. 'Hello Vida; welcome to Bar'am. I'm sure you will enjoy your time here.'

'Thank you. I hope so,' she said uncertainly.

'Leave your bag here. It will be placed in your dorm. Let's go and get that coffee.'

The two young kibbutzniks entered a large hall with many tables and chairs and a kitchen at one end. There was an urn and cups, coffee and sugar. Once they had poured their coffees they sat at one of the tables.

Vida said, 'So, when did you arrive here Adam?'

'Not long after the kibbutz opened, I arrived in June 1950.

'What brought you here?'

'It was the holocaust—as with you and so many more of our people. I was able to escape the German murders, but my family all died in Auschwitz.'

'How did you escape?' Vida asked.

'Believe it or not, a German soldier arranged for me to hide in the home of a sympathetic family.'

'I believe it. Not all Germans are evil.'

'What about you, Vida?'

'I have a similar story, as you surmised, but I'd rather not talk about it in detail right at the moment.'

'I understand.'

'Do you know the history of Bar'am Adam?' Vida asked.

'Yes, I do. This site has been occupied by the Israelites since ancient times. The Jewish people established the village of Bar'am in the 3rd century BCE. They inhabited the village continuously until the 13th century CE. Two synagogues were built of which one still stands today. The 1949 war meant that all Arabs were evicted from their homes to ensure the Israeli Lebanon border became a safe zone. Soon afterwards, the kibbutz was established.'

Joseph entered the hall indicating Vida's accommodation was ready.

Her companion smiled at her. 'It was great to meet you Vida I hope to see you at dinner.'

'It was nice to meet you, Adam.'

Vida and Joseph walked down a path until they reached Vida's new home.

There were six beds and a bathroom as well as a kitchenette.

'I'm sure you will be very comfortable here, Vida. The other girls will be back from picking fruit soon. Evening meal is at 6 pm. Tomorrow we will allocate your work routine. The concept of a kibbutz is work for free and receive accommodation and meals free.'

'Yes Joseph, I understand.'

'This is your bed. I suggest you unpack your bag before the girls return.'

Vida nodded. 'Are there any rules of the house I need to be aware of?'

'The house captain is Anna she will explain how it all works. She too is Polish and I'm sure you will like her.' He smiled. 'I'll leave you to it. I'll see you at dinner.'

'Thank you for all your help, Joseph. I really appreciate it.'

Vida unpacked her suitcase. Knowing her destination meant shared accommodation, she wasn't carrying much. There was a bedside cabinet to store her underwear and some clothes. She placed her second pair of shoes under the bed.

She had just finished unpacking when five girls entered the cabin. They all gathered and made a fuss of the new kibbutznik. They introduced themselves and asked some rudimentary questions about her journey and origin. That out of the way they all lay on their beds and rested. After a day of fruit picking they were all tired. Vida followed suit, because it had been a big day for her also.

Ruth woke the hut at 5.45 pm ready for dinner at 6 pm. The girls washed their hands and brushed their hair ready to walk down the path to the dining hall. They walked through the door at 6 pm on the dot.

The girls from the hut did not necessarily sit at the same table. Sitting at different tables gave the kibbutzniks a chance to mingle. This night was the exception and Vida's hut sat at the one table.

Vida sat next to a boy called Imre, from Hungary. He was very interested in Vida's story. In fact, all the kibbutzniks had amazing stories to tell, including Imre. When it was time to hear from Vida, she recounted how the Germans had murdered her family and that her friends and relatives had been transported to Treblinka and ruthlessly murdered. The people at the table nodded for they too had similar stories.

The next day Joseph approached Vida and explained what her duties would be.

'I have assigned you to pick apples. I will introduce you to your team leader. Just wait here and I'll go and get her.'

Joseph returned with a very pretty woman in her early twenties.

'Vida, I would like you to meet Maria She will teach you everything you need to know about picking apples.'

'Hello Vida, I'm pleased to meet you. Come with me and we'll get you started.'

Once they reached the orchard Vida began the pick, and after a full day of picking her arms felt like dead weights. At the end of each day, the kibbutzniks would swim in the Kibbutz swimming pool. That was a great reward for a day's hard work.

At dinner that night Joseph approached Vida and asked her to sit with him at the head table. There was no management group as such. Instead a system of direct participatory democracy was adopted. This was where the individual could directly influence issues and events in the community. In this mostly self-sufficient community, the collective, as well as the work ethic, played a major role.

After the meal was consumed, Joseph explained to the young woman the need to be proficient in using a high-powered rifle. The kibbutz was very close to the Lebanese border, which meant an attack by the Arabs could happen at any moment. Joseph suggested Vida should receive private lessons so that she reached the same level of proficiency as the other kibbutzniks.

Vida was a natural. Her accuracy after a short time was better than most. The rifles were kept in a gun cabinet in the cabin. Each kibbutznik had their individual rack. Ruth, the leader, held the key with a backup key held by Ruth's deputy, Sarah.

The women in Vida's hut were all sleeping soundly. After a day of picking apples, they had no trouble dreaming within a short period of hitting the pillow.

When Vida woke to the sound of gunshots, she quickly woke the other women.

'I heard gun shots close to our hut,' she said.

'Are you sure, Vida?' asked Ruth.

'I'm pretty sure, Ruth. After all, I know what a gun firing sounds like.'

'There's no need for us all to investigate,' Ruth decreed. 'Vida, come with me. Take your rifle and I'll grab mine.'

The two women opened the hut door slightly and peered out. They couldn't see anyone or anything untoward.

'Follow me,' Ruth whispered.

They crouched and began to walk to the next hut. To their horror, they discovered a girl had been shot. She was lying draped over a hedge.

Ruth indicated to Vida to slowly open the hut door. They looked in and found absolute carnage. All the kibbutzniks in that hut had been murdered.

'We need to let the others know and we'll get them to lock their doors. I'll try and get to the men's huts and let them know.'

Joseph, when informed by Ruth of the situation, mustered a group of men together to hunt down the terrorists. They discovered a hole in the perimeter fence where the gunmen cut through the wire. After searching the grounds they concluded that the assassins had disappeared back into Lebanon.

The death toll was six, all from the same hut. Their dreams of a free Israel had been cut short by Palestinian terrorists.

The entire kibbutz gathered in and around the slaughtered girls' hut despite Ruth's instruction to stay safe.

Joseph telephoned the local police chief, Shabtai Zamir, informing him of the tragedy.

'Make sure nobody enters the crime scene where there may be critical evidence. I will be there in fifteen minutes.' Shabtai hung up the phone and immediately called Isser Harek, the cabinet minister responsible for the newly created Mossad. He assigned two of his best to attend the murder scene.

'Do you know where they broke into the grounds, Joseph?' asked Shabtai.

'I think so. We found a hole in the wire fence.'

'Take me there.'

The two men walked to the spot where had Joseph found the hole. It was obvious this was where the terrorists entered.

'Let's go back and see if the Mossad officers have arrived yet.'

When they got back to the crime scene they were told the Mossad officers had entered the hut and were hoping to find incriminating evidence. All they found was five innocent kibbutzniks lying in pools of blood.

Both the police chief and Mossad gave permission for the ambulances that arrived at the kibbutz to take the bodies back to Tel Aviv where they would be buried the following day.

Mossad would use its intelligence resources to identify the terrorists and eliminate the perpetrators of this insidious crime.

The Israeli intelligence organisation had spies living in Lebanon. It didn't take them long to identify the culprits as they had boasted about their successful mission.

A team of seven highly trained Special Forces operatives crossed the Lebanese border on a moonless night in July and made their way to the village Kfar Kela where the terrorists were reputed to have lived. Mossad was confident they had identified their location.

The platoon leader, Lieutenant Colonel Daniel Sephardi, approached the villa and surprisingly he found the door unlocked. He opened the door and threw in two stun grenades. He entered, as did the six special force operatives behind him. The terrorists had been watching CNN in the front room. A fire fight ensued but after five minutes all the terrorists had been killed. None of the Israelis suffered a serious injury.

Although this action was successful it was not going to bring back the six women that were murdered by these mongrels.

Life slowly got back to normal; whatever normal was after such a tragedy.

The Kibbutzniks built a stone memorial with the names of the victims inscribed on a plaque,

EDUCATION
OF VIDA

Chapter 12

Vida had become an integral member of the Kibbutz but after several years, she began to think about her long-term future. She aspired to become a civil engineer and contribute to building the new Israel.

The university she would need to attend was in Haifa. Technion – Israel Institute of Technology was the oldest university in Israel having been established in 1912.

Haifa was an hour and a half drive from the Bar'am kibbutz, so commuting was out of the question.

Vida would need to live in a university dormitory. She discussed her conundrum with Joseph.

'Joseph, I feel this is my calling. I believe I will be able to contribute to my country's growth and wealth. On the other hand I love being part of the kibbutz and everything it stands for.'

'Vida I can understand your conundrum. We would hate to lose you, but living in a kibbutz was not meant to be a lifelong experience. You are a very intelligent woman and I believe you would make a very good civil engineer. My advice to you is go to university and get your degree.'

February 1955

Vida's good friend Adam drove her to Haifa. The journey took just under 90 minutes.

On arrival, Vida registered at the students' administration office where she was given an information pack and a book list for her first year's study. A third-year student showed her the student accommodation.

'What is your name?' he asked.

'Vida. What is yours?'

'Aleksander.'

'Really? That was my foster father's name. Are you Polish?'

'Both my parents were Polish. They escaped before the Germans invaded when I was only seven years old.'

'Do you have any siblings?'

'I had a younger sister, but she was killed in a terrorist attack at the Bar'am kibbutz a few years ago.'

'Oh my God, I was there when it happened. What was your sister's name?'

'Anna Wozniak.'

Vida felt stunned. 'She was one of my closest friends. I don't know what to say—she was a beautiful soul and I still miss her.'

'So do I.'

The two students walked side by side through the university grounds in silence. They reached the student dorms and Aleksander showed her the room she would occupy for the next three years.

Vida's Student Quarters

JORDAN LOOKS NICE

Chapter 13

November 1955

Vida not only passed her first-year exams but she became dux of her year. It had been an intense twelve months and she was looking forward to a break. Two of her fellow students had become her good friends. Derek and David met Vida at a dockside restaurant, *The Dolphin*, to celebrate their end of year.

'So, what are you guys planning during the break?' asked David.

'Nothing in particular; what about you?'

David grinned. 'Actually, I've decided on a road trip in my trusty Kombi.'

'Where exactly do you plan to travel?' asked Vida.

'I'm thinking of driving into Iraq, Syria and finally Jordan. I believe the historical sites in Iraq and Syria are something else.'

'Wow, that sounds awesome.'

'Why don't you guys come with me? The Kombi will sleep three and I could do with some petrol money.'

'When do you plan on leaving, Dave?' Vida asked.

'I've got a few things to do here, so I'm thinking in a couple of days.'

'I'll get back to you, Dave. I must admit it sounds like a great trip.'

'Me too, Dave,' Derek said. 'I agree with Vida. It sounds like a great trip.'

Derek and Vida had dinner together the next night to discuss whether they should join Dave.

'What do you think?' Vida asked. 'It could be dangerous.'

'I don't think we should worry too much about our safety. Things have been pretty quiet for a while.'

'Yeah, you're right. What the hell? I'm going. I may never get another chance.'

Derek nodded. 'I'm with you, Vi.'

When Vida and Derek knocked on Dave's door, he opened it with an expectant look on his face.

'Hello, you two. Have you decided to come with me?'

'We have,' said Vida.

'And?'

'We would love to join you.'

'That's great. I was a little worried I'd be lonely, and besides, my navigation skills aren't really up to scratch.'

The three travellers began planning their trip.

'I plan to enter Syria, where there are some magnificent historical monuments. Then I want to go to Iraq— again with fantastic historical buildings— and finally to enter Jordan and return to Israel via Aqaba.'

'That sounds like a great trip, Dave,' Derek said. 'The only point I would make is why aren't we visiting Petra.'

'I agree, Derek; Petra is on my visit list, but not this trip, because we need to get back to campus by the first of February. We just wouldn't be able to fit Petra in. Let's plan to visit next holiday.'

'Have you identified any sites yet?' Vida put in.

'The first is the closest castle to Haifa, not very far from the Syrian Israeli border. It is called Krak des Chevaliers it was a Crusaders' castle. I believe it is magnificent.'

'What's so good about it?' asked Vida.

Krak des Chevaliers

'The fortress castle was built for the Emir of Aleppo in 1031 AD. It then became the headquarters of the famous Crusader Knights Hospitaller during the 12th and 13th centuries.

'It is perhaps the best-preserved example of a crusader fortress in existence today. I understand it is an awe-inspiring example of medieval military architecture.'

The three adventurers headed off to Syria. They were all looking forward to seeing their first destination. They were suitably impressed with Krak des Chevaliers.

'I thought it was the Knights Templar that were considered the Crusader Knights,' said Vida.

'They were, Vida; the Templars were the warrior monks. The Knights Hospitaller were, as their name implies, medical monks. They did take up arms when it was necessary,' said David.

'I believe there is a camping ground a few kilometres from here so let's head there to cook up some sausages.'

'Sounds good,' Vida and Derek replied.

They found the camping ground and were delighted to discover showers and Arabian toilets i.e. a hole in the ground.

Once they had cooked and eaten their sausages they started to plan their next day. Each sipped a bottle of Al-Shark beer, Syria's finest.

'So what's next on our list, Dave?'

'The Citadel of Salah Ed-Din is only a two-hour drive from here.'

'What is it?' Vida asked.

'The Citadel of Salah Ed-Din, also known as Saladin Castle is a partly preserved Crusader fortress.'

'The Crusaders were entrenched everywhere; it's amazing they were defeated by the Muslims,' said Vida.

'It took a few hundred years before they returned to Europe with their tails between their legs.'

'So, tell us more about the Citadel, Dave.'

'The site has been used as a fortification for many centuries and is thought to have first been occupied by the Phoenicians and later by Alexander the Great. The current site was built by the Byzantines before it became a Crusader stronghold until its capture by Saladin in 1188.'

The Citadel of Salah Ed-Din

'Wow this is incredible… so Alexander the Great resided here?'

'Apparently, Vida. He got around, so they say.'

The trio slept at a camping ground not far from the Citadel.

The next morning they headed off to Iraq. Their destination was the Ahwar, a historical site made up of seven components: three archaeological sites and four wetland marsh areas in southern Iraq. The archaeological cities of Uruk and Ur and the Tell Eridu archaeological site formed part of the remains of the Sumerian cities and settlements that developed in southern Mesopotamia between the 4th and the 3rd millennium BCE in the marshy delta of the Tigris and Euphrates rivers. The Ahwar of Southern Iraq – also known as the Iraqi Marshlands – are unique, as one of the world's largest inland delta systems, in an extremely hot and arid environment.

'This is an incredible site and knowing the Sumerians lived here makes it even more amazing,' said Vida.

'I'm aware they were an ancient civilisation, but I know very little of their history,' said Derek.

'Sumer was an ancient civilisation founded in the Mesopotamia region of the Fertile Crescent situated between the Tigris and Euphrates rivers. Known for their innovations in language, governance, architecture and more, Sumerians are considered the creators of civilisation, as modern humans understand it,' said Dave.

'I don't know about you two, but I'm boiling. I think we should head down to Jordan and swim in the Red Sea,' said Vida.

'Great idea. We should hit Aqaba in about two hours,' said Dave.

The temperature in the Kombi was at least 35 degrees Celsius even with the windows open. As they approached Aqaba about fifty kilometres from the ancient city they could see the Red Sea and a pristine deserted beach.

'Take a look at that beach! Who's up for a swim?' asked Dave.

'I'm in,' said Derek.

'Me too,' said Vida.

There was a six-foot-high cyclone fence with several signs in Arabic.

ابق بعيدا

'Do you know what the signs say, Dave?' Vida asked.

'I wouldn't have a clue. Probably "Private Property" but there's no one about so we should be fine. After all we're just having a swim.'

'I'm going to go snorkelling. You never know, I might find some red coral,' said Derek.

The two men climbed the fence and reached down to Vida and helped her up. They ran down to the beach and dived into the cool water.

Derek swam out farther than the other two; he found a small reef and was fascinated with the marine life and the red coral.

He decided it was time to get back to the Kombi and once back on the beach the three adventures lay on the beach for a short while.

They soon saw what looked like an army Jeep heading in their direction. It pulled up beside them and two soldiers pointed automatic weapons at them.

They pointed to the Kombi, indicating they should get in. A soldier accompanied them, and they were instructed to drive to Aqaba.

Once they arrived, the Kombi was confiscated, and their passports were taken. They were held in a very dingy hotel under guard.

They were allowed out of the hotel for an hour a day under military guard.

A French journalist named Phillipe Hoyed became aware of the case against the three and he decided there was a story in it. He drove to Amman and contacted the British High Commissioner.

After the three had spent ten days in captivity, the court was ready to hear the case. There was meant to be an interpreter so that the accused could understand the proceedings, but he called in sick, so Dave, Derek and Vida would have no idea what was being said.

After twenty minutes, the judge banged his gavel and pronounced the three guilty of spying for Israel.

Vida was led away through a door on the left of the court, screaming her innocence. Dave and Derek were led through a door on the right.

The convicted prisoners were held in small rooms opposite each other. Dave and Derek yelled to Vida to remain strong. They were waiting for the prison van to take them to their new inhospitable home.

Aqaba Prison

The prison van pulled up and the three were about to be loaded aboard when the judge yelled out, 'Stop! They are innocent! Take their handcuffs off immediately.'

The British High Commissioner had persuaded the judge the three were merely tourists.

The judge told the group to leave Jordon immediately. The Kombi was returned to Dave and a Jeep with four Jordanian soldiers escorted them to the Syrian border in a trip which took several hours. The soldiers taunted them with their AK47s along the way.

When they reached the border post, the Jordanians turned and headed back to Aqaba with not a word spoken.

Unknown to the group Hafez al-Assad had taken the country over in a coup. There was strong resistance by the opposition and a civil war ensued.

Syria was not a safe place to be, and the Syrian police took their passports and locked them in a cell overnight.

'Talk about out of the ashes and into the fire! Which prison do you prefer— Jordanian or Syrian?' asked Derek.

Their fears were not realised because in the morning their passports were returned, as was the Kombi.

The group headed straight to the Israeli border and back to the campus in Haifa.

They all agreed the next holiday would be taken in Europe.

SUEZ CRISIS
Chapter 14

The original Suez Canal dates back to the time of the Pharaoh Senusret III (c. 1874 BC). The canal linked the Red Sea and the Mediterranean Sea via the Nile.

Senusret

Various historical leaders re-dug the canal while others let the desert envelop it. One of those leaders who saved the canal was King Darius of Persia.

During his occupation of Egypt and Syria, Napoleon Bonaparte endeavoured to build a canal that would ultimately force the English to pay the French to access the canal or to traverse the much slower land route or alternately around the Cape of Good Hope.

The project began in 1799, but it was discovered incorrect calculations meant if the canal proceeded, the Nile Delta would be permanently flooded.

Napoleon abandoned the project.

The error was rectified in 1847, allowing the Suez Canal to be built.

1858

This was the year when a French diplomat named Ferdinand de Lesseps realised his dream to commence building the Suez Canal.

Ferdinand de Lesseps

The construction of the canal would take ten years and it was officially opened on 17 November 1869.

While the canal was the property of the Egyptian government, European shareholders, mostly British and French, owned the Suez Canal Company which operated it until July 1956, when President Nasser nationalised it; an event which led to the Suez Crisis of October–November 1956.

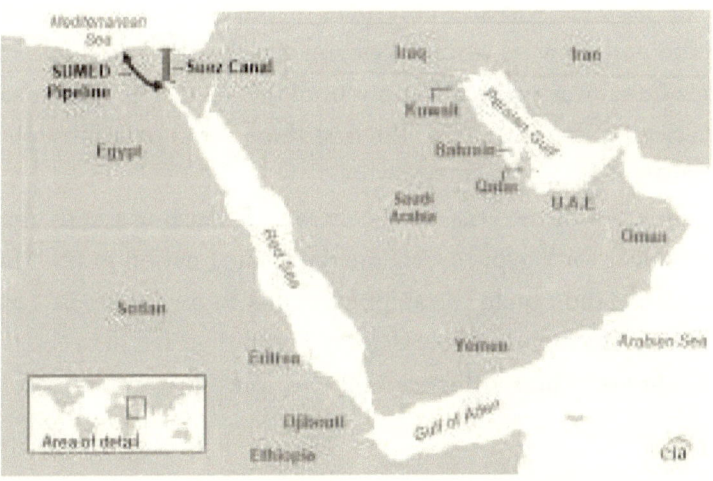

The crisis was provoked by an American and British decision to withdraw funding for the construction of Nasser's pet project, the Aswan High Dam. Nasser also closed the Straits of Tiran to all Israeli shipping. Thus the Suez Crisis began.

The reason for the decision was concern over Egypt's strengthening ties with the USSR.

The UK, France, and Israel invaded Egypt. According to a pre-agreed war plan, Israel invaded the Sinai Peninsula on 29 October, forcing Egypt to defend against the aggressor. This allowed the British and French alliance to declare the resultant fighting a threat to stability in the Middle East and to enter the war. The alliance argued they were obligated to separate the two forces but in reality, the objective was to regain the canal and bring down the Nasser government

The Canadian Secretary of State and External Affairs, Lester Pearson, was afraid the conflict would escalate into a major war involving Britain and her Commonwealth nations such as Canada.

He proposed what would be the first United Nations peacekeeping force to ensure the canal remained open. He also proposed that Israel withdraw from the Sinai Peninsula.

November 4, 1956

A majority of nations voted for Pearson's resolution, which mandated the UN peacekeepers would remain in Sinai until Egypt and Israel agreed to a withdrawal.

Significant pressure was also excerpted by the USA, and Britain finally called a ceasefire and withdrew its troops. Pearson was awarded the Nobel Peace Prize.

The Suez Canal was opened but not until the ships that Nasser sank to block access were cleared. In April 1957, the first ships could pass through the canal.

Peace returned to the Sinai Peninsula.

Nasser came out of the crisis as the victor. He became a hero among Arab nations. His object for Egypt to become the leading nation in the Middle East was realised. Israel did obtain the shipping rights to the Straits of Tiran but not the Suez Canal. Britain and France departed with their tail between their legs. Neither would regain their influence in the region.

BERKELEY
Chapter 15

December 1958

Vida completed her civil engineering degree and although she was unaware of her final grades she was confident she passed with flying colours.

The day arrived when the results were posted on the administration-building notice board. Each student had been allocated a student number at the beginning of his or her degree. Vida's number was 1952. She scoured the results and was delighted she not only passed all her subjects, but she achieved high distinctions for most of them.

The graduation ceremony was to be held on the 20th of December.

The Dean announced that Vida had been awarded the highest student award; the Ben-Gurion Award.

A week after graduation Vida received a telegram from the most prestigious civil engineering university in America, Berkeley. She had been offered a scholarship to study for a master's degree.

She knew it was a great honour, but she was reluctant to leave Israel. She decided to get advice from her good friend at the kibbutz, Adam.

She had returned to the kibbutz several times over the three years she had been studying but this time it was different.

Adam met her on her arrival they both hugged and kissed both cheeks.

'Come on, Vida let's have a coffee in the canteen.'

Once they had poured their coffee they sat outside at a table that looked out over the valley.

'So Vida what is you wish to talk to me about? I know you're secretly in love with me and want to marry me.'

'You wish. No, it's more important than that. I have been offered a scholarship at Berkeley to study for my master's.'

'Where's Berkeley?'

'In the USA. San Francisco to be exact.'

'Wow, that's incredible Vida— why do you want my advice?'

'It's a big decision. It means leaving Israel and all my friends.'

'How long would you be away for?'

'A master's only takes a year, but I may want to stay on for a doctorate and that could take up to three years.'

'Why did you decide to study civil engineering?' he asked.

'To help build a new Israel.'

'So how would studying for another three years help you do that? My advice would be to go to America, get your master's and come back home and start building.'

'You're right, Adam. I suppose my ego was getting the better of me. Thanks. I appreciate your advice.'

'Are you staying here tonight?'

'No, I need to get back to Haifa. Thanks again, Adam. I'll keep in touch.'

Vida informed Berkeley that she would be accepting their offer of a scholarship and began arranging her shift to California.

The first semester began on the 1st of February so there wasn't much time to get organised. The move wasn't as daunting as the move from Poland to Israel but nevertheless, she was nervous.

She arrived at San Francisco airport at 10 am and then caught a bus across Oakland Bay Bridge to the Berkeley campus. Vida had never seen a campus like it. It was many times larger than the Israel Institute of Technology.

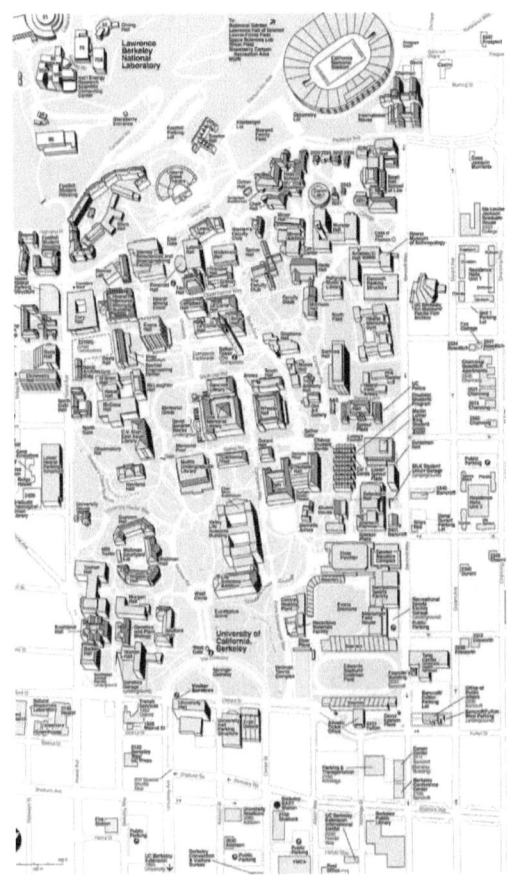

After she'd enrolled, a staff member showed her the room she would occupy in the Graduate House dorm.

Although it was bare, Vida knew she would create some atmosphere with the few personal possessions she brought with her, including a poster of Jerusalem.

Although Vida has never lived in Jerusalem she, like most Israelis, regarded the holy city as home.

Vida was due to begin her postgraduate course the following week, which gave her five days to discover Berkeley and San Francisco.

She decided to start with San Francisco for, after all, she could discover Berkeley later.

On her first day, Vida chose a tour which took her across the Golden Gate Bridge; something she had dreamed of since she was a little girl. The first part of the tour took her to Muir Woods where the giant redwoods were located. Vida couldn't get over the size of the trees.

Giant Redwoods

The bus drove to the picturesque village of Sausalito where arts and crafts and art galleries dominated the waterfront. There, she had lunch. The bus returned to San Francisco and dropped off the passengers around 2 pm.

Sausalito

Vida spent the rest of the day shopping or rather looking at what she would like to buy if she could afford it.

The next day she spent the morning on a tour of the bay including circumnavigating the infamous prison, Alcatraz. It was a very forbidding site.

The afternoon was spent window-shopping again.

The remaining three days were spent on campus familiarising herself with the grounds and facilities.

On the first morning, Vida was required to attend an assembly of undergraduates and postgraduates. They were to be addressed by the Chancellor and other senior university staff.

He welcomed the students and wished them well in their chosen fields of study.

After lunch, Vida found the lecture room where most of her group sessions would take place.

She looked around at the five other people sitting around a large table. They were all male. She gingerly took her place next to an olive-skinned, very handsome, man. The other postgraduate students seemed to know each other hence there was a conversation taking place across the table.

Vida was being ignored.

Finally, a professor entered the room. He had shaggy hair and a beard, he wore a tweed coat corduroy trousers and suede shoes.

'Hello, students, it will be my pleasure to guide you through this very important academic year. My name is John Wilson. My native state is New York, but I have resided in California for the best part of twenty years, teaching at Berkeley.

'The master's at Berkeley is conducted a little differently from other universities such as Harvard. You will work in pairs until the last month of the year when you will come together and collude.

'I will ask you to choose your partner and approach me with your names.'

Vida had no idea what to do next. She looked at the student sitting next to her, and he returned her glance.

'So, what do you think? Will we partner up?' he asked.

'Why not? My name is Vida.'

'Pleased to meet you Vida; my name is Akeem.'

'That sounds Arabic.'

'It's Palestinian actually.'

This is going to be interesting, thought Vida.

'Forgive me for asking but how did you secure a master's scholarship? Palestine is not known for its academia.'

'You mean how could a terrorist secure a scholarship at one of the best universities in the USA?'

'I didn't mean that at all. I meant it is unusual for a Palestinian to study for a Master's in Civil Engineering at Berkeley.'

'And why do you think that is, Vida? Could it be that Israel keeps us in what is tantamount to a ghetto?'

'I know what it's like to live in a ghetto. I can assure you Gaza in not a ghetto.'

'Let's drop it. We need to work together if we want to graduate,' said Akeem.

'I agree. We haven't even looked at the first assignment we need to complete.'

The two Middle Eastern students began their assignment, and as they progressed each realised the other was a highly intelligent and creative person.

By the time they completed the first assignment, "Causes Prevention and Repair of Cracks in Buildings", Vida and Akeem were beginning to build a healthy respect for one another.

Their assignment was submitted to Professor Wilson who gave them a high mark. In fact, they received the highest mark in the group.

The next assignment was 'Rectification of Building Tilt". Again the pair excelled and again received the highest mark.

'Vida, I think we should celebrate our success. How about we go out to dinner?'

'I'm up for that. Where do you suggest?'

'I believe the French restaurant *La Note* is very good. Do you like French cuisine?'

'I love it. When were you thinking?'

'How about this Saturday night?'

'That sounds good. I'm looking forward to it.'

'I'll book it…and by the way, it's my treat.'

'Don't be silly, Akeem. Let's go Dutch.'

'You can pay next time.'

'How do you know there will be a next time?'

'Because the way we are going there will be more celebrations.'

'Fair enough.'

The two engineering students met outside Vida's apartment and walked through the beautiful campus and into Berkeley Village where the restaurant was located.

'We have a reservation for two,' announced Akeem.

'Yes sir, please follow me.'

They were seated near a large window facing Berkeley Square, which was lit up to highlight the colonial architecture.

Akeem ordered a Coopers Creek Chardonnay, hoping Vida would be suitably impressed. She was.

They examined the menu and made their choices.

Vida chose Bagnat Au thon grille - Grilled tuna steak, served with aioli for her entrée.

Akeem chose Bagnat Au Poulet grille - Grilled rosemary marinated chicken breast, served with aioli and sun-dried tomato pesto

For her main course, Vida chose Poulet Au pruneaux - low simmered country style, whole-grain fed organic chicken, dried plums, garlic, and white wine, served with saffron rice and green beans.

Akeem's choice was Steak frites persillade - Grilled organic grass-fed Niman Ranch flat iron steak, with parsley butter, served with French fries.

While they waited for their meal to arrive Vida brought up the conversation of living in a ghetto.

'Akeem you equated living in Gaza to living in a ghetto. I grew up in the Warsaw Ghetto where the Germans staved us and eventually slaughtered us either by bullet or fire or by shipping us to Treblinka where my father died. It was only the kindness of a Polish family that saved me from the terrible fate of my entire family.'

'That must have been terrible, Vida, and I do emphasise but the holocaust, as tragic as it was, should not give the Israelis the excuse to kill my people; the traditional owners of the land. I was born in the West Bank and was raised in a village of Qibya. You may have heard of it.'

'No, I must admit I haven't. You say you are the traditional owners of the land, but my people lived in Israel for over 4000 years, well before you occupied it. Tell me about your village, Akeem.'

'In 1953 Israeli troops attacked my village. Over 69 villagers were killed—two-thirds of them were women and children including my mother and two sisters. The Israelis destroyed forty-five houses, a school and a mosque.'

'Why would they do that? There must have been a reason.'

Corpses from Quibya Massacre

'Yes, I'm afraid the attack was a reprisal for a Palestinian attack on a Jewish village, Yehud when Palestinians threw a grenade into a house. A Jewish woman and her two young children were killed. Still 69 nine lives for 3 was in my opinion excessive.'

Vida said, 'Our peoples must stop this violence against each other. Surely we can live in peace.'

'I hope so. Let's eat before our meal gets cold.'

Master's Apprentices
Chapter 16

As their year progressed it became clear that the two Middle Eastern students would qualify for their Master's Degree of Civil Engineering.

It also became clear that Akeem and Vida were becoming romantically attached.

They enjoyed one another's company and despite their ethnic differences and the troubles in their homeland, they became very close.

'What plans do you have when you complete your degree?' Vida asked. 'Do you intend to apply for a work visa here?'

'No, I will return to Gaza and help my people build a modern state. What about you?'

'I, too, intend to return to my homeland and contribute to the growth of a modern Israel.'

Akeem said, 'Vida, you know I love you but how can we create a life together if we live in enemy states?'

'I don't know,' she admitted. 'I love you too and I desperately wish we could build a life together but I'm afraid it would be impossible.'

'If you settled in Gaza you would be persecuted by my people, as after all Israelis are regarded as our enemies,' Akeem said.

'The same would apply to you if you married me and settled in Israel.'

'So where does that leave us?'

'We either stay in the USA or go back home and live apart.'

'We still have four months at Berkeley— let's just see what develops.'

The couple spent the remainder of their time in California studying at Berkeley and hiking through various national parks including Yellowstone in Montana where they spent a week walking throughout the day and sleeping in a two-man tent at night.

Their graduation day arrived, and Vida and Akeem graduated at the head of the class. Neither had made a final decision about their future. All they knew was that they loved one another.

They decided to have dinner at their favourite restaurant. *La Note*, and talk about their options.

'So, my love, have you decided what you are going to do?' asked Vida.

'I can't tell you how difficult it has been to decide,' he said. 'Gaza is not only my home, but an integral part of my being. I have no choice but to return and help my people.'

'I understand, darling, although it breaks my heart. I can tell you I would not be able to reside in Israel knowing you would be so close.'

'So what are you intending to do?'

'I have been offered a teaching position at Berkeley. I intend to accept and return to Israel when I recover from loving you.'

'I'm so sorry, Vida. I wish I knew another way.'

'I know, darling, you owe it to your people as I owe it to mine.'

.

Academic
Chapter 17

Vida began her teaching career at Berkeley at the beginning of 1961. Initially, she was a part time lecturer. The feedback from her students was very positive; a fact her professor noted.

Vida was asked to meet with her professor in his office towards the end of her first teaching year. She waited nervously in his anteroom.

After a twenty-minute wait, she was invited into Professor Wilson's office. Vida had been conjuring up all sorts of negative scenarios while waiting to see the professor. The one that dominated was, "sorry we have to let you go, Vida."

The reality was different.

'Hello Vida. Please sit down. I have something exciting to discuss with you.'

That's a good start, thought Vida.

'I am very pleased with your first year of teaching. I would like you to think about studying for your PhD with a teaching professorship in mind.'

'With due respect, Professor, I don't have the finances to give up teaching and study full time.'

'That's the beauty of it; you can continue teaching part time and write your thesis in your own time. The university has also offered to subsidise you.'

'Will you allow me some time to think about it?' Vida asked.

'Of course. Take your time although I wouldn't leave it too long—there are only a few Civil Engineering PhDs available.'

One concern Vida had was the fact that Akeem was due to return to Gaza in a few weeks' time. Despite the fact she would be precluded from living with him, they would be able to meet regularly.

Then again, achieving a doctorate had always been her overall ambition.

Vida made a life-changing decision. She contacted Professor Wilson and informed him of her decision.

Vida and Akeem decided to travel to New York; a city they both yearned to see.

It would be the last period they would spend together for some time.

Westside Story had recently opened so they purchased tickets to see it. They both enjoyed it very much. Apart from catching the fast lift to the top of the

Empire State building, they stayed in their hotel room, making love, and went window-shopping down Fifth Avenue.

The time came when Akeem flew back to the Middle East where he had been successful in getting a position with Abdul Salam Yassin Company; a successful Gaza-based construction company.

Vida, although missing Akeem, began her thesis in earnest. She chose "Port and Coastal Engineering" as her subject; a topic that could be of benefit to Israel.

Vida completed her thesis in eighteen months, which was regarded as a short amount of time considering she wrote it while lecturing at the university.

January 1964

Berkeley appointed her as a professor soon afterwards. She was the only female professor in the Civil Engineering school.

The Longest Six Days
Chapter 18

April 1967

Peter said goodbye to his wife Miriam after they had just eaten breakfast with their two young children ten-year-old Sam and Elisa, who was eight.

'You two enjoy school today and pay attention to your teacher. I'll see you both this afternoon.'

Peter kissed his children and his wife and headed out to his farm shed to start up his pride and joy; a 1965 John Deere tractor. Peter had a big day ahead. He was due to plough his back paddock ready to plant his crop of cucumbers.

He was halfway through the plough when a shot rang out. The Israeli farmer fell from the tractor. He had been shot through his left eye and had died instantly. The tractor was still going when Ruth and the children drove out to bring him home for dinner.

Ruth was horrified. She left the children in the car, telling them to lock the doors. She then attended to her husband. It was obvious that Peter had been fatally shot.

Ruth was undecided about what to do but she finally decided to leave her beloved husband where he lay, turn off the tractor and drive to the nearby military base and report the murder.

A colonel and four soldiers attended the scene. It was obvious that Peter had been shot with an AK47, the weapon of choice for their Arabian enemies. Further investigation discovered Syrian soldiers had murdered him.

This was the straw that broke the camel's back as it were.

Israel attacked the village of Al-Samu on the Jordanian West Bank, leaving 18 dead and 54 wounded.

In a dogfight with Syrian MiG fighters, Israel shot down six Syrian planes.

The Soviet Union provided Egypt with false information regarding Israel's intention to attack.

Egypt expelled UN peacekeepers that had been stationed in the Sinai Peninsula since the Suez conflict.

Nasser, the Egyptian President, announced the blockade of the Red Sea via the Straits of Tiran. Israel regarded this action as an act of war. Tensions between the belligerents mounted. Israel decided on a pre-emptive strike, destroying 90% of Egypt's air force on the tarmac.

The same fate awaited the Syrian air force.

Both Egypt and Syria became vulnerable to attack without air cover.

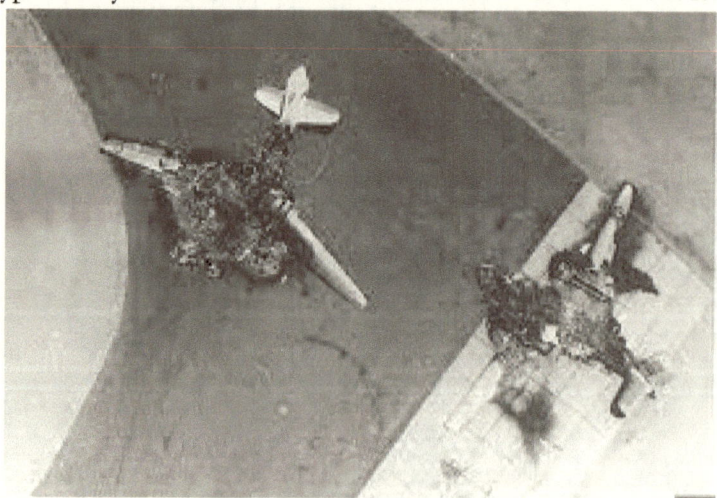

Destroyed Egyptian planes

The Israeli fighters also destroyed the Jordanian air force and now Israel controlled the skies. King Hussein of Jordan had been warned by Israel not to enter the war. He ignored their warning and paid the price.

Within three days of the destruction of its enemy's air forces, Israel had achieved a dramatic victory on the ground, capturing the Gaza Strip and the entire Sinai Peninsula up to the east bank of the Suez Canal.

An eastern front was opened after Jordanian forces began shelling West Jerusalem. Israel drove Jordan out of East Jerusalem and the majority of the East Bank.

The U.N. Security Council called for an immediate ceasefire. Israel, Egypt and Jordan agreed. Syria did not. Syria continued to shell villages in northern Israel.

On June 9th Israel launched an all-out assault on the Golan Heights, capturing the high-fortified ground. It took one day to capture it. Syria accepted the ceasefire the following day.

Israelis taking Golan Heights

Israeli soldiers celebrate their win

The Aftermath

The Arab countries that took part in the war suffered badly. Egypt suffered 11,000 casualties; Jordan suffered 6000 and Syria 1000. On the other hand, Israel lost just 700.

The amount of weaponry and equipment destroyed by the Israelis was disastrous for the Arab states. Nasser resigned in disgrace, but the people insisted that he stay.

The Six Day War created new problems for Israel as the conflict created hundreds of thousands of refugees. More than a million Palestinians were now under Israel's rule.

Vida was busy marking papers when her mail was delivered. This usually consisted of newsletters and letters from past students. She noticed an envelope with a Gaza Strip postmark. She had received letters from Akeem regularly since his return to the Middle East.

She opened it in anticipation that it may contain the news of his imminent return to the U.S.A.

Instead, it was a letter from Akeem's mother informing Vida that Akeem had been killed in the Six Day War.

She reread the letter over and over again but not a tear was spent. Finally, she let out a primal scream.

'No, it can't be my Akeem. It must be a mistake—he was an engineer not a soldier.'

Vida curled up on her office floor and began to sob. A staff member knocked on her office door inquiring if she was okay but there was no response. Jenny entered Vida's office only to find one of the university's most respected professors curled up into a foetal position crying uncontrollably.

'Professor Erzman, what's wrong?'

'Please leave me alone. I'll be okay,' sobbed Vida.

Jenny left Vida to her grief but did inform the Vice-Chancellor of the situation. He decided to leave her alone for a while and then approach her.

Akeem's death was the trigger that initiated her decision to return home. She completed the teaching year and was awarded her PhD. She arrived back in Israel in the January of 1968.

Vida had applied for and had been accepted for the position of senior Professor of Civil Engineering at Tel Aviv University.

UKRAINE
NO LONGER SAFE FOR JEWS
1905

The young Ukrainian girl was walking through a Kyiv street on her way to school. She enjoyed school and was regarded by her teachers as one of the brighter students. She could see her school in the distance.

As she approached the red brick building, six teenaged boys stepped in front of her, blocking her way.

'Where do you think you're going, you ugly Jewish bitch?'

'I'm going to school. Now please let me pass.'

'I reckon an education would be wasted on you, Jew girl.'

One of the boys pushed the girl and all the others joined in, pushing her from side to side in a circle. Finally they became sick of the torment and walked away, but not without anti-sematic jibes as they departed.

The young girl was Golda Meir, the future Israeli Prime Minister. That experience, and living through the Kyiv Pogrom in October 1906, shaped her amazing future.

The Kyiv Pogrom of 1905 came as a result of the collapse of a city hall meeting in Kyiv. As a result a wild mob was drawn into the streets. The mob comprised largely of anti–Semites proclaiming that Russia's troubles were the result of Jews. Over one hundred Jews were massacred.

Golda's family decided to leave Ukraine and immigrate to Milwaukee, Wisconsin USA in 1906 as they no longer felt safe in their home country.

It was her girlhood experiences of terror that strongly influenced her later commitment to the Zionist movement and to the establishment of a safe, secure Jewish state.

Golda completed high school, graduating near the top of her year. She then attended Teacher's College in 1917. She graduated, much to her parents' objections. They believed girls of her age should get married and have babies.

To her parents' delight Golda married Morris Myerson in 1917. She later changed her name to Meir.

1921

Mr and Mrs Myerson immigrated to Palestine, which was under the administration of Great Britain. It was a challenge living among the Arab population.

Golda and Morris joined a kibbutz, Merhavia, in the Jezreel Valley where they worked picking almonds, planting trees, looking after the chickens and working in the kitchen.

Merhavia kibbutz

Golda in the kibbutz

Golda enjoyed being a kibbutznik, but Morris did not. He fell ill, so the young couple decided to move to Tel Aviv and then on to Jerusalem where they had two children; a son named Menachem and a daughter, Sarah.

Golda secured a position with the Office of Public Works of the Histadrut, representing workers, including kibbutz workers. The organisation became the preeminent economic organisation in Israel.

1928

Golda Meir became secretary of the Working Woman Council of Palestine, serving as its representative of the Histadrut.

Histadrut was the General Organisation of Workers in Israel. Originally, it was Israel's national trade union centre representing the majority of Israel's trade unionists. Established in December 1920 in Mandatory, Palestine, it soon became one of the most powerful institutions in the Yishuv (Jews living in Palestine before Israel was established).

Golda was also a senior member of various other organisations including the World Zionist Organisation. Her activity in the Zionist political activity had begun. She was appointed as head of the political department of the Histadrut, fighting against the 1939 British White Paper, which was designed to limit Jewish immigration to Palestine. Meir organised illegal Jewish immigration to Palestine to save Jews from Nazi persecution.

Golda held various senior positions in the newly formed Israel including Foreign Minister. She secured support from the USA during Richard Nixon's presidency.

She became Prime Minister in 1968 but after the controversy of the surprise attack by Arab states in the Yom Kippur war she resigned.

YOM KIPPUR
The Day of Atonement

Chapter 19

October 6 1973

Yom Kippur, also known as the Day of Atonement, is regarded as the most solemn of Jewish holidays, observed on the 10th day of the lunar month of September or October. This is the time when Jews seek to expiate their sins and reconcile with God.

The purpose of Yom Kippur is to effect individual and collective purification by forgiving the sins of others and by repentance for one's sins against God.

Yom Kippur is marked by abstention from food, drink, and sex.

The Jacobson family comprised Abram, Sarah, Benjamin and Leah.

Abram was a senior manager with Hapoalim Bank Israel's largest financial institution.

Sarah was a high school teacher at Horev High School for Girls.

Benjamin was a conscript with the Israeli army and Leah had recently been conscripted as well.

The Jacobsons were regarded as a wealthy family living in the upmarket area of Talbiya.

The family spent the eve of Yom Kippur in quiet prayer and reflection, all dressed in white as was the tradition. This continued into Yom Kippur itself. They asked for forgiveness for past offences, which signifies God's forgiveness.

The quiet was interrupted when the telephone rang. Husband and wife exchanged glances. Who would call during this most sacred day? Finally, Jacob decided to answer it; after all, it must be important.

'Hello, this is Colonel Samuelson. I need to speak to Benjamin and Leah Jacobson urgently. I apologise for interrupting this sacred day, but it is urgent.'

Abram passed the telephone to his son.

'This is Benjamin.'

'We have been attacked by Arab forces. You need to report to barracks immediately. Your sister is required to report as well.'

'Yes sir, we will leave immediately.'

'What's happening, Benjamin?' asked Abram.

Benjamin recounted what the colonel had told him.

'How cruel— attacking our mother country on Yom Kipper! They have no respect,' said Sarah.

'It's their Ramadan as well so religion obviously means nothing to them,' said Abram.

Benjamin and Leah changed into their army uniforms and unlocked the gun locker. They had recently been allocated the Gail assault rifle manufactured in Israel.

You want war? We'll give you war.

On the 6th of October 1973, a coalition of Arab forces, including Egypt and Syria, launched a surprise attack on Israel. Israel was in the middle of their most holy of days, Yom Kippur. Making the attack even more surprising, it was Ramadan, Muslim's holy month.

The Arab forces crossed the Six Day War ceasefire lines and invaded the Sinai Peninsula and the Golan Heights. Both the USA and the USSR rushed massive supplies to support their respective allies. There was a genuine fear the two superpowers would enter the war.

The first victory for the Arab Coalition was crossing the Suez Canal.

Celebrations

The Arabian force's success was short-lived. It took Israel three days to mobilise the majority of its forces and halt the Egyptian offensive, creating a stalemate.

The Syrians conducted a coordinated attack on the Golan Heights, and they were successful in making significant gains onto Israeli-held territory. After three days of heavy fighting, Israel pushed the Syrians back to the original ceasefire lines. Once that objective was achieved, the Israelis launched a four-day-long counter-offensive deep into Syria. Within a week Damascus came under fire.

Egypt mounted another attack against the Israelis, which was repulsed and which resulted in Israel counterattacking and crossing the Suez Canal into Egypt. Troops began advancing on Suez City. Casualties were heavy on both sides.

A ceasefire came into force on October 22, which was brokered by the United Nations, but it didn't last the day. By October 24, the Israelis had progressed, circling the Egyptian Third Army and Suez City, bringing them to within 100 kilometres of Cairo. There was a real fear that the United States and the Soviet Union would become involved physically in the war.

A second ceasefire came into play and the war was declared over.

The Yom Kippur war had implications for both the Arab nations and Israel.

The Arabs, although declared the losers, took to heart their early successes; unlike in the 1967 war.

The Israelis became aware that they might not always win these wars.

It was this recognition that led to the Israeli-Palestinian peace process.

The Camp David Accords saw Israel return the Sinai Peninsula to Egypt, resulting in the Egyptian-Israel peace treaty. Egypt was the first Arab country to recognise Israel. The Soviet Union lost all influence in the Levant.

Sadat, Carter and Begin

GAZA
Chapter 20

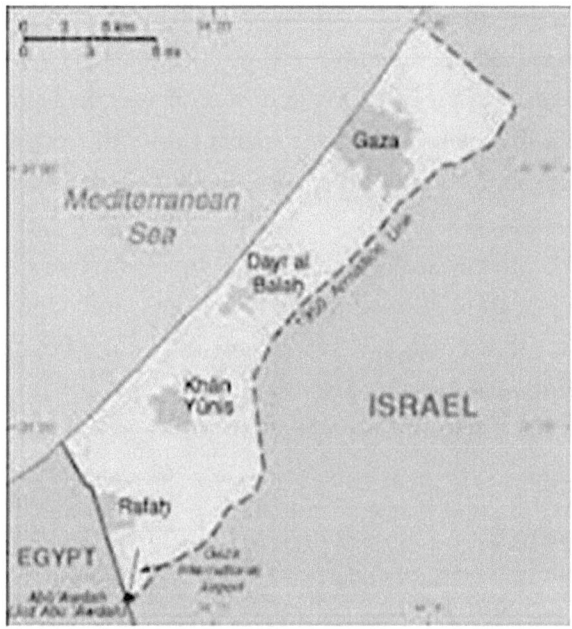

Gaza city served as Egypt's administrative capital of the Levant; consequently the Egyptian governor located his residence in the region.

The camel caravans used Gaza as a major stopping point.

Gaza became a military power involved in various wars between Egypt and Syria.

The Bible mentions Gaza as the site where Samson was imprisoned and met his death destroying the temple.

The first Israelite conquest of Gaza was during King David's reign in the 11th century BCE. Gaza became part of the Kingdom of Israel.

Gaza was conquered and ruled by many peoples, including those of Assyria, Egypt, Persia, Greece and the Bedouins.

Gaza was occupied by Israel during the Six Day War in 1967. Although Israel had occupied Gaza, the Palestinians executed the administration and limited government of the territory.

The Israeli military was known to interfere in the country's administration to control violence.

There was no love lost between the Palestinians and Israelis, with armed struggles against Israel becoming endemic between 1969 and 1971. The Israeli Defence Forces, under the command of Ariel Sharon who later became Prime Minister of Israel, largely crushed these insurrections.

It has been estimated that 90% of Arab terrorism was directed against Arabs that were employed by Israeli companies. The retaliation by Israel was fast and merciless. Gaza was not a safe place to be.

1972

Vida enjoyed her role as a Professor of Civil Engineering at Berkeley. It was satisfying to observe her students graduating and going on to enter the workforce and helping to build structures around the world.

She thought of Akeem every day. He had asked her to marry him the day he departed for the Middle East.

'Vida, I have a question for you, my love.'

'Oh, and what might that be, my Arabian prince?'

'Will you marry me?'

'Oh Akeem; I love you with all my heart, but...'

'But what?'

'Do you mean marry you and settle in America or do you mean Gaza or Israel?'

'You know I mean Gaza. The reason I studied Civil Engineering was so I can help rebuild my country.'

'Akeem, with me being Israeli it would be very difficult for you and me to live there. Let me think on it for a little while.'

'So your answer is neither yes nor no, but maybe?'

'Let me think on it.'

The couple hugged and kissed before Akeem caught a cab to the airport.

RELUCTANT SOLDIER

Chapter 21

Akeem was born to a Jordanian mother and a Palestinian father, and he and his three brothers lived in Amman with their mother and father.

Akeem's father Amir was a high school teacher and his mother, Emna, was a nurse.

Akeem excelled at school and his ambition was to become a civil engineer.

The family was regarded as middle class and as such could afford an annual holiday. The holiday Akeem remembered most was visiting Petra. The ancient ruins intrigued him.

Petra is an ancient city located in the centre of the Hellenistic period. The Hellenistic period is defined with the death of Alexandra the Great and the Roman period. Petra is located in southwest Jordan. It is pierced by the Wadi Musa (The Valley of Moses). Tradition has it Moses struck a rock with his staff and water gushed out.

Roman Amphitheatre

The Treasury, Petra

Remains have been discovered from the early stone age (Palaeolithic) and the Bronze Age.

The Arab tribe, the Nabataeans, appeared in the sixth century BC in Petra where they settled. They expanded into the Levant, eventually making Bosra in Syria their capital.

Bosra

Akeem's father accepted a teaching post in Gaza. The family was excited about the move as at that stage Gaza was living in peace.

Akeem continued to excel in school and was accepted for a scholarship at Berkeley in California.

It was there he met Vida.

January 1972

Akeem decided to fly to Amman initially and catch up with his extended family, consisting of six uncles and aunties and thirty cousins. He travelled under a Jordanian passport.

It had been a long time since Akeem stepped onto Jordanian soil. He was only ten when the family moved to Gaza.

He disembarked the Boeing 747 and entered the arrival lounge. The line to customs was long and it took him twenty-five minutes to reach the customs officer.

'Good morning, Mr Ahmed; welcome home.'

'Thank you. It's good to be back.'

'Are you returning to complete your compulsory military service?'

'No, my home is now in Gaza. I am here to visit my family.'

'You are a Jordanian citizen, and you are compelled to do your duty.'

The customs officer called over a security guard.

'Can you escort Mr Ahmed to the customs office please? When I process the remaining passengers I will interview him.'

Akeem waited nervously in a small claustrophobic office. The temperature outside was 36C, and this little office was not air-conditioned, so it was stifling.

Akeem could not believe what was happening. All he wanted to do was visit his family and he now regretted not going straight to Gaza via Jerusalem.

The Jordanian customs officer entered the room.

'Now Mr Ahmed, do you understand why you have been retained?

'Not really. I live in Gaza, not Jordan, so why should I be obligated to serve two years in the army?'

'You are a Jordanian citizen and as such you must complete two years of national service.'

'So what happens now?'

'A military escort will take you to the Royal Jordanian Army Base in Amman. Don't worry; you won't be lonely. There are 60,000 reservists stationed there.'

Within the hour two soldiers arrived and escorted Akeem back to their army base. He was required to give his personal details, which included any qualifications. The officer conducting the interview was quite obviously impressed that Akeem was a civil engineer with a Master's.

'We need engineers in our ranks. You will be kept busy; I can assure you.'

The new recruit was escorted to his barracks, which he would share with forty other conscripts.

For the next six weeks he was required to run ten kilometres daily with full pack. He also learned how to shoot a British manufactured L1A1 automatic rifle.

L1A1 Rifle

Jordan used British made weaponry from tanks to fighter aircraft.

Akeem and his new army friends noticed a buzz around the camp no one was sure why. The soon learned that they would all be involved in an attack on Israel.

The Jordanian army needn't have worried; they would mostly be out of harm's way.

After the thrashing they received in the Six Day War, King Hussein decided not to open a third front against Israel during the Yom Kippur war.

The king's compromise was to send troops to support the Syrians and to placate the Arab world.

It has been rumoured that Jordan and Israel had an agreement to keep the conflict symbolic.

Jordan supporting Syria was considered to be a lesser of two evils; Israel avoided attacking Jordanian troops. They promised Israel they would act cautiously, but Jordon did lose soldiers during the conflict. This was inevitable.

The king personally informed the U.S. ambassador in Amman that the participation of Jordanian soldiers in the war was just part of the facade presented to other Arab countries.

One of the Jordanian soldiers to lose their lives was Akeem Ahmed.

Akeem was killed in Syria.

He was awarded the Star of Honour posthumously for his bravery in battle.

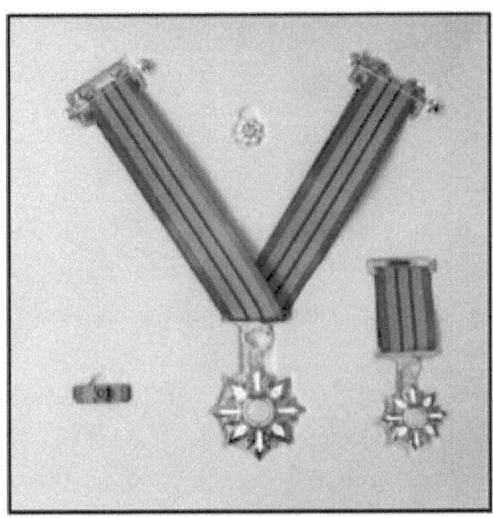

A NEW LIFE
Chapter 22

1993

Vida had been teaching at Berkeley for thirty-two years. She had been head of the department for the past fifteen years and was due to retire in 1995.

She had never married because, although she had several relationships, she never got over Akeem.

She had recently decided to reside in Gaza City when she retired, hoping to fulfil Akeem's dream of rebuilding the city.

She felt it was the right time to go as the Oslo Accords were in place, giving Palestine the administration of the Gaza Strip plus Jericho. The Israeli troops withdrew, leaving the newly formed PLO in charge.

Gaza's leader was Yasser Arafat, who became the leader of Fatah. He, along with Shimon Peres and Yitzhak Rabin, was awarded the Nobel Peace Prize in 1994.

1995

Vida arrived at Ben-Gurion International Airport on January 1st. Although she had returned home several times since her move to America, she knew very few people. Most of her friends had either died or immigrated to other countries such as Australia.

The Dean at Berkeley was Jewish, and he knew many high-ranking government officials in Israel. He also knew Yasser Arafat as he was on the selection committees for the Nobel Peace Prize. Vida carried with her several letters of introduction, which she hoped would make the path to Gaza easier.

She booked herself into her favourite hotel, the Setai, At close to $800 it was an extravagance, but it was worth it.

Vida relaxed around the magnificent pool and ate in the Michelin three hat restaurants.

She felt no guilt for she knew that when she entered Gaza, luxury would be the last thing she would encounter.

January 5

When Vida checked out of the hotel, a Land Cruiser provided by her new employer was waiting for he to take her into Gaza City. The trip of about 70 kilometres would take an hour.

She had searched the Internet and found a one-bedroom apartment in Rimal, right on the beach.

The company Vida joined was Abdul Sakam Yassin, a well-respected construction company. Vida was impressed with their reputation for building schools and hospitals. The company also built desalination plants.

She had a week to settle into her apartment and purchase appropriate furniture and groceries. Her apartment was close to the company's offices, which meant she could walk to head office.

She naturally arrived on time on her first day. She had received instructions to meet with the company's president, Abdul Sakam Yassin, who was also the organisation's founder.

The receptionist asked Vida to take a seat. She offered Vida a tea or coffee, which Vida declined.

After a twenty-minute wait, the receptionist instructed Vida to enter the president's office. She was surprised at how rudimentary it was. He didn't rely on opulence to impress his guests.

'Miss Erzman, please take a seat. I've been looking forward to meeting you.'

'Thank you, sir. It's a pleasure to meet you.'

'You have joined our firm as a senior executive. My other executives call me Abdul, so please do the same.'

'Thank you, Abdul, and please call me Vida.'

'Vida, you have a very impressive resume. You could have worked anywhere in the world, so why did you choose Gaza of all places? After all you are an Israeli citizen.'

Vida explained her relationship with Akeem and how she hoped she could realise his dreams.

'That's a very noble cause, Vida. We have received a commission to build an annex to the Gaza City hospital. I would like you to be the civil engineer in charge of the building.'

'That would be an honour, Abdul—when do I start?'

'Tomorrow.'

'Hit the ground running as it were.'

'No time like the present, Vida. I'll have the plans available later today. In the meantime, I'll introduce you to the team and show you your office.'

It won't be much of an office based on the president's, she thought.

Vida was presently surprised to find her office was quite large and had views over the Mediterranean Sea.

The commercial plans were delivered to Vida's office soon after lunch. The annex would house 200 beds and forty operating theatres; a sizeable project.

Vida would be responsible for ensuring pollution would be kept to a minimum to protect the Gaza environment.

She was responsible for minimising the construction cost, at the same time ensuring occupational and safety standards were kept up. Local zoning laws needed to be adhered to.

Her most critical task was to supervise the construction, ensuring the workmanship was of the highest standard and that the development met the expectations of the stakeholders.

Collaboration with the project manager required excellent communication.

Vida was dedicated to the hospital project, working sixty-hour weeks, and sometimes more. The timetable allowed for two years, but with Vida's dedication and a dedicated and skilled workforce the construction was completed in twenty-two months.

Yasser Arafat officially opened the hospital, thanking Vida and others for their work.

Vida was committed to constructing significant buildings in Gaza, including university buildings, schools and shopping centres; all designed to improve the lives of the Palestinian people living in Gaza.

Life was good. She made many friends and was a respected member of the community, despite being an Israeli.

2006

Everything changed in 2006. Elections were held in Gaza. Fatah was expected to win and continue its rule, but Hamas took control of the Palestinian National Council and the conflict between Israel and Gaza was reignited.

Israel bombed Gaza in an air ground assault codenamed Operation Summer Rains. This was as a result of rocket attacks into Israel and to secure the release of an Israeli soldier captured by Hamas.

Over 15,000 rockets were fired from Gaza into Israel in 2006.

The other significant event in 2006 was the 2nd Lebanon War.

The war was initiated when Hezbollah conducted a cross border raid. They fired rockets into Israeli towns so as to divert attention away from an attack on two armoured Humvees that were patrolling the border. The attack resulted in three soldiers being killed. Hezbollah also captured two Israeli soldiers, taking them back to Lebanon.

A rescue attempt was foiled with five more soldiers losing their lives.

Hezbollah attempted to organise a prisoner swap, but the Israelis refused to cooperate.

Israel's answer incorporated airstrikes and heavy artillery targeting Lebanon. A significant target was the Rafic Hariri International Airport and various civilian areas were also hit. An air and naval blockade was also initiated.

Hezbollah responded with massive rocket attacks and guerrilla attacks in northern Israel.

The casualty count was 1,300 Lebanese and 165 Israelis.

Vida was concerned that her life in Gaza would change for the worse under the rule of Hamas. She had witnessed the conflicts between Gaza and Israel, and she regarded both as her own. What she didn't anticipate was her arrest.

INCARCERATED
Chapter 23

January 2007

Vida was in her office going over the plans for a new school, when her assistant knocked on her door.

'Vida, there are two men demanding to see you.'

'Who are they, Jamal? I'm very busy and I don't remember any meetings being scheduled.'

'They are both wearing military uniforms and insist on meeting with you immediately.'

'Oh, I see. Show them in, Jamal. I've got a feeling I won't enjoy this.'

The two Hamas soldiers entered Vida's office.

'Ms Erzman I am placing you under arrest.'

'What is the charge?'

'Being an Israeli spy. Place your hands behind your back.'

Vida's wrists were handcuffed

She was blindfolded and led outside where she was placed in the back seat of a Land Cruiser with the two soldiers sitting one on either side. Two more were in the front, including the driver. She was then driven to the woman's prison on the outskirts of Gaza City.

She was processed and given an orange prison uniform. She was then placed in a solitary confinement cell; a place with no windows or light. It was here that Vida was kept for several weeks, unable to leave even for a shower.

Vida requested that she be given the opportunity to call her boss or a lawyer, but her request was denied.

Finally she was released from her cell and placed in a large cell with twenty other women. There were a few murderers and thieves but they were mostly women who had sex while being single.

Six months passed before she received notice that her trial would be held on July 1st. She didn't have access to any legal council, despite facing the death sentence or at least a long time in jail.

The trial was held behind closed doors and lasted two hours. The prosecution argued that as an Israeli citizen living in Gaza she must be a spy. They could not present any supporting evidence.

The judge found Vida guilty. He did not pronounce the death sentence on the grounds that Vida had contributed to the growth of Gaza despite her spying activities. He sentenced her to fifteen years in the women's prison.

As the prisoner was led away, she thought, so this becomes my life.

Vida underestimated the Palestinian legal system. When she arrived back at the jail she was returned to solitary confinement. Her sentence included twelve months in solitary.

Vida's Cell

Without any books or magazines, Vida began to make up stories, hoping she would remember them and convert her stories into books upon her release.

Her stories covered love, war, and her life both in the USA and the Middle East.

2006

Hamas seized an Israeli soldier, Gilad Shalit, inside Israeli territory near the Gaza border and imprisoned him to be used as a bargaining chip.

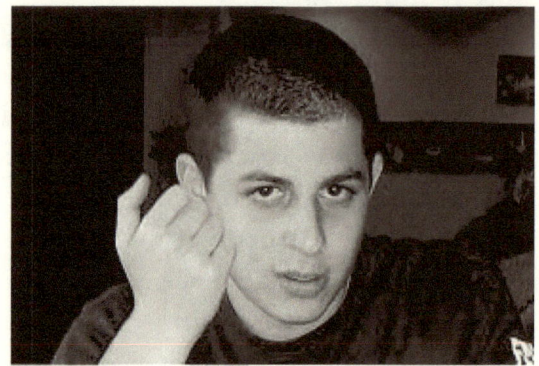

Gilad Shalit

2011

Hamas and the Israeli government came to an agreement regarding a prisoner swap.

Hamas would release Gilad Shalit in exchange for 1027 Palestinian prisoners.

Vida was woken early by two female guards. They handcuffed her and escorted her to a waiting Land Cruiser. She was blindfolded.

'Why am I here?'

'You'll find out soon enough,' answered one of the guards.

Vida was hopeful she was being transferred to another prison. The other option was that her sentence had been changed and she was to be executed.

The Land Cruiser stopped next to an Israeli check point. Vida stayed inside the vehicle while one of the guards entered the checkpoint.

Vida had become a last-minute inclusion in the prisoner swap at the insistence of Benjamin Netanyahu, the Israeli Prime Minister.

Thirty minutes later, Vida was being taken to a safe house escorted by IDF soldiers. The euphoria she felt was amazing. The next day a government car picked her up and drove her an unknown location.

Knesset

She was escorted by a lieutenant colonel; Vida wondered where they were heading and why such a high-ranking officer was her escort. She soon found out as the Land Cruiser pulled up in front of the Knesset.

The officer assisted her from the vehicle and led her into the impressive building where finally they entered the anteroom of the Prime Minister.

They didn't have to wait long before another army officer invited Vida into the Israeli leader's office.

Prime Minister's Office

Mr Netanyahu rose from his desk, greeting Vida with a warm handshake.

'Ms Erzman, we meet at last. I have followed your career for many years.'

Vida was flabbergasted. Why had the Israeli Prime Minister followed her career? In fact, why was he even aware of her existence?

'I am honoured Mr Prime Minister how did you know about me?'

'I studied architecture at MIT from 1972 through to 1976. You were a Professor of Civil Engineering at Berkeley with a reputation for innovation. I studied some of your research papers.'

'Oh, I see. As I said earlier, I'm honoured.'

Mr Netanyahu got down to business. 'How were you treated in Gaza?'

'Considering the circumstances, it was reasonable, although two periods in solitary confinement were very difficult.'

'I understand the charges against you were that you were an Israeli citizen living and working in Gaza.'

'Yes, that was pretty well it. I helped construct hospitals and schools and various other buildings, but they discounted that as propaganda.'

'Why did you live in such a hostile environment?' he asked.

'My fiancé was Palestinian and a fine civil engineer. He was killed in the Six Day War. I felt it was my duty to help his people, not in war or in terrorism, but to help them rebuild their country.'

'Yes, I can understand your reasoning. Well. Welcome home, Vida, if I can call you that.'

'Please. And thank you for orchestrating my release, sir.'

'It was my pleasure. Are you intending to continue your work here?'

'I'm not sure. I think I need to settle into life in Jerusalem first.'

'I understand. It was a pleasure to meet you, Vida. I hope we meet again.'

'It was also a pleasure to meet you, Mr Prime Minister.'

Vida exited the PM's office to where the officer was waiting to take her back to the safe house.

As her escort approached her safe house, a hail of Hamas rockets filled the sky. The vehicle pulled over to the side of the road.

Vida looked up, to see the Israeli Iron Dome take out most of the rockets. Israeli ingenuity wins again she thought.

Iron Dome is an air defence missile system developed by two Israeli firms with support from the U.S. Emphasis is on defence. It is never used to attack or to retaliate and poses no threat to Palestinians.

The system has three components: a radar that detects incoming rockets; a command-and-control system that determines the threat level; and an interceptor that, if the system determines human lives or infrastructure are at risk, seeks to destroy the incoming rocket before it strikes.

According to Israeli officials, it is about 90% effective in stopping short range rockets fired by Hezbollah terrorists next door in Lebanon or Hamas and Islamic Jihad terrorists in neighbouring Gaza. The system protects Israelis of all backgrounds and faiths.

For example, when Hamas and Islamic Jihad fired more than 4,300 rockets from Gaza into Israel, more than 1,500 targeted heavily populated areas, including Israel's largest city, Tel Aviv. Iron Dome shot down more than 90% of those rockets, greatly reducing the death toll. Even with Iron Dome, about a dozen Israelis were killed. That number would have been much higher without Iron Dome.

August 18 2011

Vida was well aware that she might have leaped out of the frying pan into the fire by moving to Jerusalem. She contemplated moving back to the USA where she held dual citizenship, but she decided to live the rest of her days in Israel, the land of the Jews, her people.

She had just eaten her lunch when she turned on the television to watch "Jerusalem News".

There was a report of a series of cross border attacks by twelve Palestinian militants in southern Israel on Highway 12 near the Egyptian border.

There were additional Israeli soldiers stationed in the area as the Israel Security Service had alerted the government that an attack was inevitable.

The first attack was on a passenger bus travelling down Highway 12 near Eilat.

Israeli Bus Bombed

The next attack, ten minutes after the first, was a bomb explosion next to an Israeli army patrol.

The final attack involved an anti-tank missile aimed at a family car, killing all four passengers.

It was reported that eight Israelis were killed and several militants.

Vida was saddened by the television report.

When would this violence end?

THE HOUSE THAT BEN BUILT

Chapter 24

December 2011

Vida received a telephone call from the Prime Minister's office requesting she attend a meeting with Benjamin Netanyahu.

She was curious as to why the PM would want to meet with her so soon after the initial meeting.

A government car was arranged to pick Vida up and bring her to Knesset where she was shown into the Prime Minister's office upon arrival.

'Hello, Vida great to see you again. Please take a seat. I have something to discuss with you.'

Vida sat on the lounge waiting to hear why she was once again with the Prime Minister.

'Vida, I am about to embark on a very exciting project, and I am keen to get your opinion.'

'I will do my best, sir.'

'I have purchased four apartments on the top floor of a building in the Jerusalem District. My intention is to combine all four into one apartment fit for a prime minister with the appropriate security measures built in. I'm aware that to do so would entail significant engineering consultation. I would like you to oversee the construction. What do you think?'

'Who have you appointed as your architect, sir?'

'Someone I trust implicitly.'

'Excellent. You need to trust your architect. Who have you chosen?'

'Me.'

'Of course. Have you designed the apartment?'

'I have.'

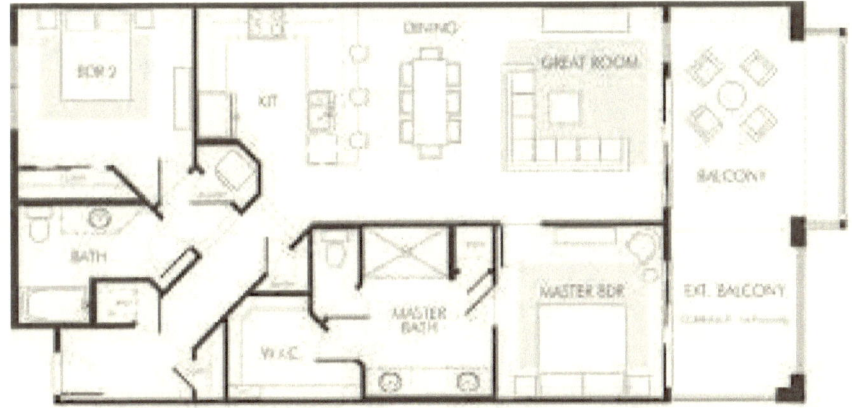

'What are the dimensions?'

The prime minister said, 'Five hundred square metres all up.'

'That's a sizeable apartment,' Vida pondered.

'Yes. I need your engineering expertise to ensure it will be structurally sound.'

'It is difficult to tell, having not seen it, but I would assume some structural work will be required. The fact that you are combining four separate apartments will mean supporting walls will be replaced with steel structural beams.'

'That's why I need your help, Vida. Are you prepared to take on the project?'

'I would need to inspect the building before committing. However, all things being equal, I would be honoured, Mr Prime Minister.'

'If we are going to work closely on the project I suggest you call me Benjamin, at least in private.'

Vida insisted she must inspect the building alone for she didn't want any outside influences attempting to affect her judgement.

She concluded that the renovation was possible with proper structural support. She requested a meeting with Benjamin to discuss her plan and an estimate of costs.

'What do you think of my proposed penthouse?' he asked.

'I am impressed with the architectural drawings. Your apartment will be quite magnificent.'

'I'm sure there is a proviso, Vida. How much structural work will need to be done and at what cost?'

'I can only estimate the cost, but I believe $200,000 would be a fair budget.'

'That's within my budget. When can you start?'

'Why don't we agree to beginning in the first week in March?'

'Excellent, Vida, I expect you have not included your consulting fees in your estimate?'

'Correct, Benjamin. I charge $1000 a day.'

He nodded. 'My people will draw up the contract and you get your lawyers to review it. Then we can get moving.'

'Sounds like a plan.'

March 3 2012

Vida had arranged to meet with the building contractor on site. Benjamin had used him on a previous project in Tel Aviv some time ago.

Vida waited for him in apartment one.

A big man with a barrel chest greeted her.

'So, you must be Vida the engineer. My name is Levi the builder.' He chuckled. 'Sounds like Thomas the Tank Engine, doesn't it.'

'Or Bob the Builder. I'm pleased to meet you, Levi. No doubt we will get to know each other very well by the time this project is complete.'

'Yes, I'm sure. Don't be too tough on me will you?'

'You do your job and I'll do mine and I'm sure everything will work out fine.'

Levi and Vida worked well together along with the tradesmen in Levi's company.

The renovation took four months and came in slightly over budget at $220,000, due to skylights being added to the design.

Benjamin Netanyahu was very happy.

WHEN WILL THIS BLOODY CONFLICT END?

Chapter 25

Vida continued her career consulting on various projects in Israel and the United States, Her love of both Israel and Palestine did not diminish but the continued conflicts saddened her greatly.

Friday, March 11

Tamar Fogel was a normal Jewish girl living with her family in the West Bank community of Itamar. On Friday March 11 she returned home from a Sabbath youth activity playing games and learning about the Jewish faith.

When she arrived home she discovered the front door was closed, although her parents normally left it open for her.

Tamar opened the front door, looking into the front room suspiciously. The house was a complete mess. Furniture had been turned on its side and some had been smashed.

As she moved through the house searching for her family, she found a pool of blood and then discovered the bodies of her two younger brothers, eleven-year-old Yoad and four-year-old Elad.

Tamar was in shock as she entered her parents' bedroom only to find her mother and father dead on the floor. What horrified Tamar even more was the discovery of her three-month-old sister stabbed while asleep in her crib beside her parents' bed.

Tamar was relieved to find her brothers eight-year-old Ro'ie and two-year-old Yishay who had been able to hide from the terrorists.

The police identified two suspects; cousins Amjad and Hakim Awad who confessed to the murders.

The two terrorists were members of the Popular Front for the Liberation of Palestine. They had spent considerable time planning the attack, choosing a Friday night when Jewish families would be home celebrating the Sabbath.

Unable to secure guns, the two carried machetes, masks, and wire cutters. They were able to scale the security fence and crossed 500 metres of no man's land until they reached the first row of houses.

They broke into the first house. There was no one home and they were able to steal a gun and ammunition.

They heard children's laughter from the next-door house, so they broke in and slaughtered the Fogel family.

On April 14, 2011, a raid led to the arrests and the discovery of the guns.

Trial and Conviction

Although the court had the power to sentence both men to death it decided not to, despite the extreme nature of the attack.

On 5 June 2011, Amjad and Hakim Awad were indicted before the Judea and Samaria Sector Military Court on five counts of murder, stealing weapons, breaking and entering, and conspiracy to commit a crime. The suspects confessed to the murder and the military prosecution in the case presented forensic evidence linking them to the scene of the crime, including DNA samples and fingerprints. Hakim and Amjad described what they did with self-control and did not express regret over their actions at any stage of the investigation.

On 16 January 2012, both terrorists were sentenced to five life terms and an additional seven years in prison.

PEACE?

Chapter 26

This past century in some ways has been a century of war and bloodshed. It has seen a year by year increase in defence spending by most countries in the world. If we are to change this trend we must seriously consider the concept of non-violence, which is a physical expression of compassion. In order to make non-violence a reality we must first work on internal disarmament and then proceed to work on external disarmament. By internal disarmament I mean ridding ourselves of all the negative emotions that result in violence. External disarmament will also have to be done gradually, step by step. We must first work on the total abolishment of nuclear weapons and gradually work up to total demilitarisation throughout the world. In the process of doing this we also need to work towards stopping the arms trade, which is still very widely practiced because it is so lucrative. When we do all these things, we can then hope to see in the next millennium a year by year decrease in the military expenditure of the various nations and a gradual working towards demilitarisation. Human problems will, of course, always remain - but the way to resolve them should be through dialogue and discussion. The next century should be a century of dialogue and discussion rather than one of war and bloodshed.

The Dalai Lama 2000

Using the same weapon as David

2000
The new century continued on in violence

2000: The second intifada, or Palestinian uprising, began after riots broke out following a visit by right-wing Israeli political figure Ariel Sharon (and later prime minister) to a compound in Jerusalem venerated in Judaism, Christianity and Islam (The Temple Mount). Clashes and other violence continued until 2005, leaving hundreds dead on both sides.

Palestinian supporters of the Islamic group Hamas celebrated their victory in the Palestinian parliamentary elections during a rally in Gaza City on Jan. 27, 2006.

2006: The Palestinian militant group Hamas won elections in Gaza, leading to political strains with the more moderate Fatah party controlling the West Bank.

Israeli warplanes retaliated for rocket fire from Gaza pounding dozens of security compounds across the Hamas-ruled territory in unprecedented attacks from airstrikes.

December 2008: Israel began three weeks of attacks on Gaza after rocket barrages into Israel by Palestinian militants. The rockets are supplied by Egypt using tunnels. More than 1,110 Palestinians and at least 13 Israelis are killed during the confrontation.

November 2012: Israel killed Hamas military chief Ahmed Jabari, touching off more than a week of rocket fire from Gaza and Israeli airstrikes. At least 150 Palestinians and six Israelis were killed.

Summer 2014: Hamas militants killed three Israeli teenagers who were kidnapped near a Jewish settlement in the West Bank, prompting an Israeli military response. Hamas answered with rocket attacks from Gaza. A seven-week conflict left more than 2,200 Palestinians dead in Gaza. In Israel, 67 soldiers and six civilians were killed.

December 2017: The Trump administration recognised Jerusalem as the capital of Israel and announced that it planned to shift the U.S. Embassy from Tel Aviv, stirring outrage from Palestinians.

2018: Protests took place in Gaza along the wall with Israel, including demonstrators hurling rocks and gasoline bombs across the barrier. Israeli troops killed more than 170 protesters over several months. In November, Israel staged a covert raid into Gaza. At least seven suspected Palestinian militants and a senior Israeli army officer were killed. From Gaza, hundreds of rockets were fired into Israel.

May 2021: After weeks of tension in Jerusalem which led to Israeli police raiding al-Aqsa Mosque, one of the holiest sites in Islam, Hamas fired rockets towards the city for the first time in years, prompting Israel to retaliate with airstrikes. The fighting, the fiercest since at least 2014, saw thousands of rockets fired from Gaza and hundreds of airstrikes on the Palestinian territory, with more than 200 killed in Gaza and at least 10 killed in Israel.

December 2008: Israel began three weeks of attacks on Gaza after rocket barrages into Israel by Palestinian militants. More than 1,110 Palestinians and at least 13 Israelis were killed.

The **2022 Gaza–Israel clashes** lasted from 5 to 7 August 2022. The Israel Defence Forces (IDF) conducted some 147 airstrikes in Gaza and Palestinian militants fired approximately 1,100 rockets towards Israel.

MODERN ISRAEL
AN ECONOMIC POWERHOUSE

Chapter 27

Israel's economy can be described as a developed free-market economy.

Israel is regarded as an advanced economy with a sophisticated welfare system and a significant military machine reputed to possess nuclear weapons.

The country has developed a high technology industry second only to Silicon Valley.

Another significant metric is the number of start-ups. Israel rates second largest in the world with only the USA ahead of it. It rates third in the number of NASDAQ listed companies after the U.S. and China.

Israel has attracted multinational companies such as IBM. Google, Hewlett-Packard, Cisco, Facebook and Motorola to create development centres as well as Intel, Microsoft and Apple creating research and development facilities.

Israel's diamond industry is one of the largest in the world amounting for 23.2% of the country's exports.

Israel is resource poor and imports petroleum, iron and other raw materials but recent discoveries of natural gas off its coast will make a difference.

Solar power has become another industry that Israel can rely on for its energy requirements.

Israeli Solar Plant

Statistics

Currency	Israeli new shekel (ILS;
Fiscal year	Calendar year
Country group	• Developed/Advanced[• High-income economy
Population	9,521,000[
GDP	• $520.700 billion (nominal, 2022 est •
GDP growth	• 3.4% (2018) 3.5% (2019) • 2.2% (2020e) 8.2% (2021e) 5.0% (2022e
GDP per capita	• $54,690 (nominal, 2022 est • $50,200 (PPP, 2022 est
GDP by sector	• Agriculture: 2.4% • Industry: 26.5% • Services: 69.5% • (2017 est
Inflation (CPI)	−0.59% (2020 est.

Population below poverty line	0.35% (2021 est 3.1% (2022 est. 17.9% (2017)
Human Development Index	• 0.919 very high (19th) • 0.814 very high IHDI (2019
Labour force	• 4,065,500 (May 2020) • 59.0% employment rate (May 2020
Labour force by occupation	• Agriculture: 1.1% • Industry: 17.3% • Services: 81.6% • (2015 est
Unemployment	• 3.5% (May 2022 • 6.0% youth unemployment (Q1-2020 • 143,800 unemployed (May 2022
Main industries	high-technology goods and services (including aviation, communications, telecommunications equipment, computer hardware and software, aerospace and defence contracting, medical devices, fibre optics, scientific instruments), pharmaceuticals, potash and phosphates, metallurgy, chemical products, plastics, diamond cutting, financial services, petroleum refining, textiles
Ease-of-doing-business rank	35th (very easy, 2020)
Exports	$115.57 billion (2019 est
Export goods	Cut diamonds, refined petroleum, pharmaceuticals, machinery and equipment, medical instruments, computer hardware and software, agricultural products, chemicals, textiles and apparel.[15][16]
Main export partners	• United States 28.8% • United Kingdom 8.2% • Hong Kong 7% • China 5.4% • Belgium 4.5% •
Imports	$108.26 billion (2019 est.
Import goods	Raw materials, military equipment, motor vehicles, investment goods, rough diamonds, crude petroleum, grain, consumer goods.
Main import partners	• United States 11.7% • China 9.5% • Switzerland 8%

131

- Germany 6.8%
  - United Kingdom 6.2%
  - Belgium 5.9%
  - Netherlands 4.2%
  - Turkey 4.2%
  - Italy 4%
- (2017

FDI stock	$82.82 billion (2011 est.; 43rd)
Gross external debt	$97.463 billion (July 2019 est.;)
Public debt	59.8% of GDP (2018 est.; 28th)
Budget balance	−3% of GDP (2011 est.; 105th)
Revenues	$68.29 billion (2011 est.)
Expenses	$75.65 billion (2011 est.)
Economic aid	**Received-**
	$4.81 billion as US Foreign Aid
	Donated-
	$0.28 billion as Israeli foreign aid
Credit rating	• Standard & Poor's: • AA− • Outlook: Stable[• Moody's: • A1 • Outlook: Positive[• Fitch: • A+ • Outlook: Stable
Foreign reserves	$201.694 billion

MODERN PALESTINE
GAZA & WEST BANK

Chapter 28

GDP per capita in the Palestinian territories rose by 7% per year from 1968 to 1980 but slowed during the 1980s. Between 1970 and 1991 life expectancy rose from 56 to 66 years, infant mortality per 1,000 fell from 95 to 42, households with electricity rose from 30% to 85%, households with safe water rose from 15% to 90%, households with a refrigerator rose from 11% to 85%, and households with a washing machine rose from 23% in 1980 to 61% in 1991.

Economic conditions in the West Bank and Gaza Strip, where economic activity was governed by the Paris Economic Protocol of April 1994 between Israel and the Palestinian Authority, deteriorated in the early 1990s. Real per capita GDP for the West Bank and Gaza Strip (WBGS) declined 36.1% between 1992 and 1996 owing to the combined effect of falling aggregate incomes and robust population growth. The downturn in economic activity was due to Israeli closure policies in response to terrorist attacks in Israel, which disrupted previously established labour and commodity market relationships. The most serious effect was the emergence of chronic unemployment. Average unemployment rates in the 1980s were generally under 5%; while by the mid-1990s it had risen to over 20%. After 1997, Israel's use of comprehensive closures decreased, and new policies were implemented. In October 1999, Israel permitted the opening of a safe passage between the West Bank and the Gaza Strip in accordance with the 1995 Interim Agreement. These changes in the conduct of economic activity fuelled a moderate economic recovery in 1998–99.

As a result of the Israeli blockade, 85% of factories were shut or operated at less than 20% capacity. It is estimated that Israeli businesses lost $2 million a day from the closure while Gaza lost approximately $1 million a day. The World Bank estimated the GDP of the territories at US$4,007,000 and of Israel at US$161,822,000. These numbers are respectively US$1,036 and US$22,563 per year per capita a significant difference.

For 30 years, Israel permitted thousands of Palestinians to enter the country each day to work in construction, agriculture and other blue-collar jobs. During this period, the Palestinian economy was significantly greater than the majority of Arab states. Until the mid-1990s, up to 150,000 people—about a fifth of the Palestinian labour force—entered Israel each day. After the Palestinians unleashed a wave of suicide bombings, the idea of separation from the Palestinians took root in Israel. Israel found itself starved for labour, and gradually replaced most of the Palestinians with migrants from Thailand, Romania and elsewhere.

In 2005, the Palestine National Authority (PNA) Ministry of Finance cited the wall whose construction began in the second half of 2002, as one reason for the depressed Palestinian economic activity. Real GDP growth in the West Bank declined substantially in 2000, 2001, and 2002, and increased modestly in 2003 and 2004. The World Bank attributed the modest economic growth since 2003 to "diminished levels of violence, fewer curfews, and more predictable (albeit still intense) closures, as well as adaptation by Palestinian business to the contours of a constrained West Bank economy". Under a "disengagement scenario" the Bank predicted a real growth rate of −0.2% in 2006 and −0.6% in 2007.

In the wake of of Israel's withdrawal from Gaza there were shortages of bread and basic supplies due to closure of the al Mentar/Karni border-crossing into Israel. Israel's offer to open other crossings was turned down by the Hamas-run Palestinian authority.

Following the elections held in 2006 which was won by Hamas…

The Quartet, set up in 2002, consists of the United Nations, the European Union, the United States and Russia. Its mandate is to help mediate Middle East peace negotiations and to support Palestinian economic development and institution-building in preparation for eventual statehood. It meets regularly at the level of the Quartet Principals (United Nations Secretary General, United States Secretary of State, Foreign Minister of Russia, and High Representative of the European Union for Foreign Affairs and Security Policy) and the Quartet Special Envoys.

The Quartet cut all funds to the PA led by Hamas. The PA had a monthly cash deficit of $60 million-$70 million after it received $50 million – $55 million a month from Israel in taxes and customs duties collected by Israeli officials at the borders. After the elections, the Palestinian stock market fell about 20%, and the PA exhausted its borrowing capacity with local banks. Israel ceased transferring $55 million in tax receipts to the PA. These funds accounted for a third of the PA's budget and paid the wages of 160,000 Palestinian civil servants (among them 60,000 security and police officers). The United States and the

European Union halted direct aid to the PA, while the US imposed a financial blockade on PA's banks, impeding the transfer of some of the Arab League's funds. In May 2006, hundreds of Palestinians demonstrated in Gaza and the West Bank demanding payment of their wages. Tension between Hamas and Fatah rose as a result of this "economic squeeze" on the PA.

In 2009, the Israeli military removed its checkpoint at the entrance of Jenin in a series of reductions in security measures.[1] In September 2012, EU activists stated that the Palestinian economy "lost access to 40% of the West Bank, 82% of its groundwater and more than two-thirds of its grazing land" due to the occupation and settlement construction.

The first planned Palestinian city named Rawabi is under construction north of Ramallah in the West Bank with the help of funds from Qatar In 2013, commercial trade between Israel and the Palestinian territories was valued at US$20 billion annually.

Rawabi

President Biden announced new contributions totalling $316 million to support the Palestinian people. This is on top of the more than half a billion dollars the United States has provided to the Palestinian people since the Biden Administration restored much needed funding to the Palestinians.

Since 2000, the European Union has allocated €852 million in humanitarian aid to help Palestinians in need. In the Gaza Strip, EU funding provides vulnerable families with cash assistance, helping them cover their basic needs, including safe education for children and health care.

Population	4,569,087 (2018)
GDP	$10 billion (2012 est.
GDP growth	• 1.2% (2017) 0.9% (2018)
	• −2.5% (2019e) 2.1% (2020f
GDP per capita	• $1924 (West Bank
	• $876 (Gaza
GDP by sector	• Agriculture: 5.5%
	• Industry: 23.4%
	• Services: 71.1%
	• (2014 UN data
Inflation (CPI)	2.7% (June 2013
Population below poverty line	25.8% (2011 est.
	•
Labour force	• 1,316,023 (2019
	• 32.0% employment rate (2018
Labour force by occupation	• Agriculture: 12%
	• Industry: 23%
	• Services: 65%
	• (2008
Unemployment	27.5% (Q1 2013
Main industries	Cement, quarrying, textiles, soap, olive-wood carvings, mother-of-pearl souvenirs, food processing
Ease-of-doing-business rank	117th (medium, 2020
Exports	$720 million (2011
Export goods	Olives, fruit, vegetables, limestone, citrus, flowers, textiles
Imports	$4.2 billion (2011
Import goods	Food, consumer goods, construction materials
Public debt	$4.2 billion (June 2013)
Budget balance	$1.3 billion (13% of GDP; 2012 est.)
Revenues	$2.2 billion (2012 est.)
Expenses	$3.54 billion (2012)
Foreign reserves	$464 million (march 2016) (163nd)

May there be peace at last in the Holy Land.

The End

ACKNOWLEDGMENTS

Preview Readers
Martin Humphries
Ian Jones
Editor
Sally Odgers
Anna Shearer, my wife (when's he going to stop writing)

BIBLIOGRAPHY

G   colonels in israeli army 1973 - Google Search   https://www.google.com.au/search?q=colonels+in+israeli+army+1973&source=hp&ei=NDmx'

W   History of Israel - Wikipedia

   Golda Meir Biography - life, family, childhood, children, parents, name, story, death, school, information, born

   New Tab

   Golda Meir (1898-1978) - UWM Libraries

   The house where Golda lived - The Jerusalem Post

   Golda Meir, Israel's Fourth Prime Minister (1969–74) on JSTOR

W   History of Gaza - Wikipedia

   Hamas: The Palestinian militant group that rules Gaza - BBC News

   Life inside Gaza's only women's prison | Crime | Al Jazeera

wix   Website | Wix.com

   FUTURE RELEASES | Mysite

   Today We Remember: The Fogel Family Massacre | IDF

√   Victims of Palestinian Violence and Terrorism since September 2000 | Ministry of Foreign Affairs

   September 28, 2000: Ariel Sharon Visits the Temple Mount, Sparking the Second Intifada | The Nation

Roman Empire. Jews In Roman Times | PBS

Pompey's Siege of Jerusalem - Livius

Timeline for the History of Jerusalem (4500 BCE-Present)

Timeline of Roman history - Wikipedia

Timeline of the Palestine region - Wikipedia

The Cold War for Kids: Suez Crisis

semaphore_suez_canal_history_and_significance_0.pdf

Suez Crisis | Definition, Summary, Location, History, Dates, Significance, & Facts | Britannica

December 2015 UC Berkeley Commencement Address | Office of the Chancellor

Best Civil Engineering Assignment Topics to Score A+ in Academics

Milestones: 1945–1952 - Office of the Historian

Timeline of the Israeli–Palestinian conflict - Wikipedia

Qibya massacre - Wikipedia

Yehud attack - Wikipedia

California Guided Hiking Tours - Sierra Nevada / Yosemite / Sequoia — International Alpine Guides

timeline of arab israeli wars - Google Search

Six-Day War | Definition, Causes, History, Summary, Outcomes, & Facts | Britannica

Yom Kippur | Holiday, Purpose, Meaning, & Facts | Britannica

Yom Kippur War - Wikipedia

How to Celebrate Yom Kippur: 10 Steps (with Pictures) - wikiHow

Why were the Philistines and the Israelites always at war? | GotQuestions.org

(7) Quora

(85) (PDF) Combat cuties: photographs of Israeli women soldiers in the press since the 2006 Lebanon War | Eva Berger · Academia.edu

(12) History & Mystery. Oh My!

History of the Israeli–Palestinian conflict · Wikipedia

Saul - Bible, King & Israel · Biography

David and Goliath | Bible Story

Saul - Wikipedia

Daily Life in the Warsaw Ghetto WW2 | Imperial War Museums

What was the History of the Jewish People? – Shalom from G-d – English

Crusades · The First Crusade and the establishment of the Latin states | Britannica

The Project Gutenberg E-text of The Story of the Crusades, by E. M. Wilmot-Buxton

André de Montbard · Wikipedia

did Hugues de Payens fight in the holy land · Google Search

Hugues de Payens | Deadliest Fiction Wiki | Fandom

Hugues de Payens · Wikipedia

Hugues de Payens | Assassin's Creed Wiki | Fandom

Hugues de Payens | PDF | Knights Templar | High Middle Ages

Jerusalem captured in First Crusade · HISTORY

Crusades: Definition, Religious Wars & Facts · HISTORY

G   historical fiction books about the levant · Google Search

W   History of Israel · Wikipedia

S   What was the History of the Jewish People? · Shalom from G-d · English

a   Davidic Line Today: Ask the Rabbi Response

P   Muhammad: Legacy of a Prophet | PBS

S   What was the History of the Jewish People? · Shalom from G-d · English

C   Brief History of Israel and the Jewish People

H   Palestine · HISTORY

W   David · Wikipedia

  The Story of King David in the Bible · Jewish History

S   In the hills of Haifa, a 500,000-year-old home with a view · Haaretz Com · Haaretz.com

G   israel 20,000 bce · Google Search

•••   Israel dig unearths prehistoric 'paradise' · BBC News

▪   Humans in Israel during the Ice Age! Jaw and rodent fossils challenge belief about when man first arrived there – The Jewish World

G   king david's life · Google Search

  Yom Kippur War: Grand Deception Or Intelligence Blunder

a   29 Reconstructed Faces Of Ancient People From Neanderthals To Jesus

R.   Israel archeologists find that early cavemen ate bone marrow

  It's Complicated: The Path of an Israeli-Palestinian Love Story · The New York Times

V   I Fell in Love with an Israeli Soldier – La Voce di New York

I Fell in Love with an Israeli Soldier – La Voce di New York

In the hills of Haifa, a 500,000-year-old home with a view - Haaretz Com - Haaretz.com

Timeline of Jewish history - Wikipedia

Qesem Cave excavation reveals prehistoric man ate tortoises 2 Feb 2016

Hebrew Boy Names | Mama Natural

Neanderthals could hear and produce speech like humans, scientists say

Bronze Age 'New York' discovered, Israeli archaeologists say | News | DW | 06.10.2019

En Esur - Wikipedia

Newly-discovered Ancient City Was the "New York City" of Its Day – Dusty Old Thing

bronze age in israel - YouTube

Early Bronze Age City Was the 'New York' of the Southern Levant | Smart News | Smithsonian Magazine

Bronze Age Swords (Sword Finishing)

Jericho | Facts & History | Britannica

what year did the was of jericho come down - Imali Yahoo Search Results

History of the ancient Levant - Wikipedia

Home and Family · Canaan & Ancient Israel @ University of Pennsylvania Museum of Archaeology and Anthropology

Palestine - The Iron Age | Britannica

Archaeology of Israel - Archaeological Time Periods - Iron Age/Israelite Period | Iron Age Israelite Period

Who Invented Steel: A Look at the Timeline of Steel Production

Warfare in Ancient Israel and the Importance of Iron

First published 2023 by Crabtree Pty Ltd

Middle Earth: The Levant is a work of fiction. Any resemblance to real persons, living or dead, is purely coincidental.

ISBN: 978-0-6451166-8-7 (p/b)
ISBN: 978-0-6451166-9-4 (ebook)